THE BRAND NEW
BAUGHER WESTERN

C-BAR

THE C-BAR RANCH
WESTERN ADVENTURE
SERIES

BOOK 4

MARK BAUGHER

Copyright © 2018 by Mark Baugher
Published by Dusty Saddle Publishing

ISBN-13: 978-1724460509

ISBN-10:1724460501

All rights reserved. No part of this publication may be reproduced, distributed, or transmitted in any form or by any means, including photocopying, recording, or other electronic or mechanical methods, without the prior written permission of the publisher, except in the case of brief quotations embodied in critical reviews and certain other noncommercial uses permitted by copyright law.

Other Books & movies by Mark Baugher

Six Bullets Series

Volume 2

Westerns

Cimarron Frost – Bounty Hunter

Motion-Pictures

C- Bar

Have you checked out the official c-bar website **and** Youtube channel**?**

A NOTE FROM M. ALLEN

I have enjoyed this new "C-Bar" Western adventure from the ever-talented Mark Baugher, just as I have enjoyed all the books that preceded it. Baugher has a style that is hard to explain. He is unlike any other writer in his ability to bring the Wild West to life in front of your eyes. I would say that the majority of Western readers will enjoy this new adventure—and I hope they are inspired to write a Western of their own.

- *M. Allen – bestselling Western author of the top thirty smash hit "<u>A Sheriff To Kill For</u>" and many others.*

A NOTE FROM JOHN D. FIE, JR.

I have to say that I am a competitive writer and sometimes I find myself rising to the challenge against my fellow author. I like to think that this challenge helps writers to turn out better stories. While reading this new "C-Bar" adventure, I decided that I just needed to up the ante and start work on my next book. The high quality of this new release made me want to get to work on my next adventure—and once I'd finished this excellent story, that's what I went off to do.

- *John D. Fie, Jr. – bestselling Western author of the top ten smash hit "<u>Cattle Queen of the Pecos</u>" and many others.*

A NOTE FROM ROBERT HANLON

Baugher has something going on that makes him an excellent reading choice. His ability to tell a story is second to none, his ability to turn his books into movies seems to be a key factor to his success—but he has soul, and that soul allows him to draw in a reader and keep them excited for the whole duration of a book. This new one is the fourth book in his fabulous "C-Bar" series—it's a pleasure for me to say that it's one of the best he's ever written. Enjoy!

- *Robert Hanlon – bestselling Western author of the many hits including his current top twenty bestseller "Tin Star."*

C-Bar

Introduction

We are born into this world and we also die in this world. If we laugh and love in between, it's all worth it.

I'm Chris Babb. Let me continue to tell you about my life, living with the Barnetts on the C-Bar Ranch, my favorite place on Earth.

Life was settling down at the C-Bar. My adopted daughter, Liz, continues to be more comfortable. Right now, I am looking at something that might be the cutest thing I have ever seen. Little Liz is completely mesmerized with my cousin, Jessie Lynn. Liz and I got to the house for dinner, arriving before JL. She was playing with Dez and Mac and having fun like only little girls can do. JL walked in. Little Liz stopped and stared. Didn't move—just stood there, staring.

I could understand why. JL is probably five foot six inches tall. Blond hair, blue eyes, tan and thin from hard work. Of course, she has a big hat, and a white shirt with no suspenders. Us men need something to hold up our pants, but JL has hips for that. She has a gun on her hip with her pants tucked into her high-topped boots. Little Liz couldn't take her eyes off JL.

JL walked over, swept her up and sat at the table with Liz on her lap. All the while Liz just stared. Now that I'm a father, I pay attention to things like this. The person Liz will model after is JL, and I'm damn glad of it. This makes me rest easier. I also know that JL would fight a bear to protect her. Believe me, I will take and need all the help I can get to get this little girl a good start in life.

When I'm lying in bed at night and worrying about Liz, I think about the life she has here on the C-Bar. This ranch is alive with family members. Even those who are not related are considered family. I mentally go through the list. Uncle Dockie. He's a rough old bird until his family is concerned. It's hysterical to see him melt when family come around. Go to town and people step aside and give him respect. See him at home, and he is being taken advantage of all day long.

Then there is Aunt Marsha, a sweet and honest woman no matter where she is. Dez, Mac and Little Liz live for her attention and don't believe for a second that anyone else will do. It's Aunt Marsha or nothing. It doesn't matter how hard I try, they will go for her every time. Truth is, it's not just the kids, it's everyone.

Then there is Eric Alan. He is truly a nice man. Reminds me of his mother, Aunt Marsha. If he is sitting and trying to read, the girls will wallow all over him. He doesn't say anything, just moves his head around trying to see past them and continues reading.

I've already told you about JL, no need to go over that again. Brandy Lynn lives on a ranch nearby. She and Clay Boy are raising Ned. Talk about a lion protecting its cubs! Brandy Lynn is ferocious. Clay and Ned are as nice as people come. They laugh a lot and play music and sing in town.

Then there is me. I'm stuck in this position of fatherhood with Liz. I have to be responsible. For her own sake, I have to say things like 'no.' I have to worry about her safety and manners. Hey, she has to learn from someone, and I guess it's me. Aunt Marsha told me it's more important to be a parent then a friend. I know she is right, but damn, I don't like being resented by this little girl. Uncle Dockie gives me some wisdom from time to time. This is the latest: *When my kids wanted something, they knew their mother was the best place to get it done, but when they were in trouble they came looking for me. We all have our place and they need different things so just be glad you have your value.* I sure am glad I have some older folks to make me feel better.

I won't even get into all the uncles. They lie with every breath to impress the girls with how wonderful they are.

Dez is a sweet little girl. Quiet most of the time and very sensitive. I sometimes see her just staring off and pondering. She reads before she goes to sleep. I have a connection with her that I value. Sometimes we just look at each other and smile. Every now and then, I say or do something that makes her laugh. I never know when it will happen, but I enjoy it a lot.

Then there is Mackie. Bold is an understatement. No such thing as a stranger. There are times when she can aggravate me and times when I roar with laughter over her antics. On one occasion, I saw her causing trouble.

She looked at me and our eyes met. She just smiled at me as if admitting she knew what she was doing. On another occasion, we were all sitting on the porch one day when an unknown rider rode up. He was a cattle buyer. He said, "Any cattle on this ranch for sale?" Mackie responded with "Who's askin?" Aunt Marsha got after her for being rude but Uncle Dockie, JL and myself found it very amusing. Eric Alan just shook his head.

Chapter 1
What to Do with the Money?

Since our successful cattle sale, we had some money. We were debt free, and you would think that we would be happy and carefree. Not so. What do we do with our money? This was weighing heavily on all of us when Eric Alan called a family meeting. We all gathered around the kitchen table as Eric Alan stood up and began speaking.

"What we do now will determine the future for us and the kids. I have been thinking about this a lot. Here is what I suggest. We learn from our mistakes. No more borrowing money. We damn near lost the ranch doing that. We are debt free now and have cash hidden away. However, we don't live any different. We live and act poor and hoard the money. The day will come when a neighboring ranch or cattle herd is for sale, and we make an offer. Here is the rule. If we ain't stealing it, we don't buy it."

Then Uncle Dockie said, "That don't seem fair to me."

Eric Alan was ready for him. "That's why you ain't doing any of the negotiations. That will be for us younger folks to worry about. We need to think about the fact that everything goes up and down. Good times and bad both come in their own time. We never buy during good times. That's buying at the top of the market, and that is bad business. We wait for everything to look bad and then we buy. When things are going good, we all think it will continue, and when things are bad, we think that will never change. But it does. From now on, we buy during bad times and sell during the good. We got young people to think about. Any questions?"

Everyone was quiet. Then Uncle Dockie said, "Are you saying that I don't have to worry about this anymore?"

"Yup," said Eric Alan.

Uncle Dockie smiled from ear to ear. He looked like a man with the world lifted from his shoulders. Then it was my turn.

"You all know that I own Uncle Phylo's ranch. I have filed the deeds turning ownership of that ranch over to the C-Bar. Everything and everyone I value in the world is right here. The C-Bar just doubled in size. So if anyone wants to protest, just shut up. It's done and over."

Uncle Dockie stood up and said, "We should pay you for it. That don't seem fair to me."

Everyone was shaking their heads and that turned into laughter.

Then Mackie replied, "Nothing for you to worry about Pa-Pa. Remember what you just said?"

C-Bar

That made people laugh even harder.

Mark Baugher

Chapter 2
Dockie Learns to Read

Most days the men and JL were out away from the house doing what we do. I left Little Liz with Aunt Marsha. She kept the girls at the house, keeping them busy with chores and school work. Uncle Dockie was learning to read with the girls. He never had the opportunity for what he calls book learning. Every day he sat at the kitchen table with them and buried his head in a book. Quite a sight—a wrinkled, leather-skinned older man surrounded by little girls, poring over a book. His forehead became scrunched up with concentration. His lips moved with every word. He would call out to the girls for help with a word. They then sat and figured it out together. It was an amazing thing to witness. He told me that it's as if there was a world out there he didn't know about. He was obsessed with Mark Twain. Twain was a new author. Aunt Marsha bought The Adventures of Huckleberry Finn in town. I saw Uncle Dockie pick it up, part the pages and put his nose in between the paper and breathe deeply. Dez asked him why he did that, and he said he just loves the smell.

I walked in and they were all too busy to give me any attention, but Aunt Marsha greeted me.

"Good morning, nephew. How are you today? Want some coffee?"

"Of course, I do. Thank you."

I was staring at Uncle Dockie when Aunt Marsha said, "Quite a sight seeing all this happen. I never really knew if Dockie could learn like this."

I frowned as I looked at Aunt Marsha.

"Don't worry, Chris. He can't hear me."

I whispered, "He's right there."

Aunt Marsha continued, "Let me tell you a little something about you men. You can only think about one thing at a time. It would take a gunshot to bring him out of that book."

I probably had a dumb look on my face.

"Sit down, nephew, and let me fill you in. Men and women are different. Men focus on one thing and do it best when something is some distance out in front. When they look around they will move their head and not their eyes. Dockie has been protecting us all with that very trait. It's a man thing. If I send him to the pantry for a can of something, he will walk over and look inside. He won't see it until he backs up a foot or two."

Now I realized this was something you don't learn in school, so I asked, "Well, okay, tell me about you women."

Aunt Marsha continued, "We are different. We focus

up close. We can see from side to side without moving our heads. We can also do more than one thing at a time. I can cook, help with studies, settle an argument and talk with you all at the same time."

I think my head was cocked sideways because Aunt Marsha giggled at me.

"Dockie's world is out there, and my world is in here. That's what it takes for us to survive. That's also why Dockie and JL are so formidable out on the trail. They have all directions covered."

"Well, Aunt Marsha, all the time I thought you were just smarter than us."

She gave a hearty laugh. "You are very right about that. Well, about some things anyway."

Mark Baugher

Chapter 3
Old Trouble

Life was good. The mood around the ranch was lighthearted. Kids were growing and keeping us all amused. The lifting of the financial pressure felt like a new world opened up. People whistled while going about their business. How could things get any better?

I was walking to the house when I met a grim-looking Uncle Dockie, JL and Eric Alan. They were strapping on their guns and walking toward the horse corral. I grabbed JL and asked her what the big problem was.

"Nothing, cuz. It don't concern you."

I wasn't about to let this go. "JL, everything what goes on around here is my concern. Start talking!"

She looked at her pa and brother. Uncle Dockie said, "We just got word that Big Mike is back in town. Says when he finds you, he's going to kill you."

That was a shock for me. From time to time, I wondered if he would come back, seeking revenge. The first time we met, I knocked him out with that chunk of firewood; the second time in Tombstone, Wyatt pistol-whipped him. A man like Big Mike don't forgive or forget. I was lucky twice, and he probably planned on a fair fight this time, which meant I stood very little chance of survival. He may have been a big oaf, but he wasn't stupid.

"Wait a minute! This is my problem, and I will kill my own snakes."

Uncle Dockie rolled his eyes. "I knew we shouldn't have told you."

"Let me get saddled up and ride to town."

JL was shaking her head. "Cuz, you ain't going without us."

I knew better than to argue. We were all saddled and leaving when Aunt Marsha came running out with her shotgun. She handed it to me and I didn't protest, I took it. It was a long ride to town, and it gave me time to think.

When we rode in, people were staring at us. I'm sure the word was out, and they were expecting us. We rode past the sheriff's office. Behan was just coming out. He acted like he didn't see us. We took the horses to the livery. David Caldwell took and tied up the horses. I could tell he wanted to say something, but he didn't. Us walking across the street had to be a little bit scary for the townsfolk. Four of us all abreast and no smiles among us.

The saloon was full of people. JL walked in first with a grim look on her face. A drunk made some comment and she hit him with her pistol butt so fast it was a blur. Down he went. Uncle Dockie was right behind her. No one would look at him; it was obvious he was there for war. Eric Alan was next. He looked at the bar and several people moved away to make room. All three of them put their backs to the bar. I was last in, carrying Aunt Marsha's shotgun. I heard someone say, "Oh, Lord, it's Chicago Chris."

At that moment, I was appreciating my falsely-earned reputation. My eyes were adjusting, and I scanned the barroom. Much to my disappointment, there he was, sitting at a poker table. His friends left pronto, then he was alone. I walked over to him, threw my shotgun on the table and sat down. We stared at each other for a while and then he spoke.

"Well, well, if it ain't the Chicago Kid. You must have heard that I wanted another go at you. Problem for you is that I'm ready this time. Are you prepared for me to break your back?"

Now, I knew that he was one bad son of a bitch. He lived to make people afraid of him. That kind of sick mentality was extremely dangerous.

In the calmest voice I could muster, I said, "Big Mike, you don't kill easy. I am impressed. Here is what happens today—no matter if I live or die, my family will kill you. They know better than to let you live and then have to look over their shoulders. This will end today. Maybe for both of us."

I was relieved to see a slightly different look on his

face. Problem was he was in front of a barroom full of people. To back down would shame him, and he won't let that happen. I leaned forward and spoke softly so only he could hear.

"Big Mike, I don't want to fight you. I would be a fool to want to. I have a little girl to think about. Things have changed for me. However, I can be your best friend or your worst enemy. I would rather be your friend. You're a big, mean, son of a bitch and having you for an enemy is not a smart thing to make happen."

He liked me showing him respect, and I could see him soften up a little bit.

"So what's it going to be, Big Mike? Are we friends or do we both die today?"

Big Mike pondered, "Just how do we get out of this problem and not lose respect from everyone watching?"

My relief was flowing. I didn't give a damn in hell about the room's respect, so I thrust out my hand first. He slowly put out his huge bear paw and we shook hands. You could feel the room sigh in relief. When you have ridden a lot of horses, you soon learn that every now and then you get a horse that wants to be the boss and will damn sure fight you for the privilege. Here is how that goes—fight him to the bitter end. Do whatever it takes for him to give up that desire. What you have then is an outstanding horse. They are fearless and loyal. Damn fine horses.

"Big Mike, you are known far and wide for being a good hand. Would you like to work on the C-Bar again?"

He wasn't ready for that. I could tell he was thinking hard about it.

"Well, Chicago Chris, I need a job real bad. I would come back to the C-Bar under one condition—don't hit me with a chunk of firewood again."

We both laughed as the crowd watched, wide-eyed.

"Come out tomorrow and start work. You know our routine."

Big Mike responded, "I'll be there about sunrise."

I stood up and walked out of the bar. My people were right behind me. We mounted up and left town. About twenty minutes out, JL slugged me in the arm.

"Well, dammit, cuz, what happened?"

I knew I had her then. I never got tired of tormenting JL.

"Not much. I just hired Big Mike. He starts tomorrow."

It was a long ride home, but I got everyone convinced

Mark Baugher

to give him a try. Ain't life full of surprises?

Chapter 4
Big Mike Was Back

Big Mike was there and ready to go at sunrise the next day. When Frying Pan Charlie started cooking, Big Mike was patiently waiting at the table. The crew eyed him with concern until I walked in.

"Boys, Big Mike is one of us again. Let's all give him a break and let him prove himself."

There were a few grunts and groans, but no-one said much, except Mike.

"You men have good reason to doubt me. I ain't here to cause trouble. All I want is a good place to work and be a good hand. Maybe I growed up some since you last seen me. Something about a chunk of firewood and a bath in the river got my attention."

The mood lightened up. People were smiling and kidding him. The men started shaking his hand and welcoming him back. People are quick to forgive, especially those of us who remember our young years and flinch at some of the things we did.

After eating, everyone walked toward the corrals to work with some young horses. As we passed the main house, Uncle Dockie, JL, Eric Alan and Little Mackie were on the porch. I've told you before how Little Mac can talk up and we never know what she is going to say. She watched us walk by.

"Are you Big Mike?"

He stopped and looked at her. Now, remember, he was a huge man and she weighed a good sixty pounds soaking wet. He just nodded his head.

"You don't look so tough to me."

We all went quiet. Then Big Mike said, "What be your name?"

With a sober face, she responded, "My name is Mac. Why you asking?"

Big Mike started to grin. Then he started to laugh. This set us all off. We were all reinforcing her rude behavior, but we just couldn't help it. This was funny. Eric Alan just shook his head like only a father can do. I noticed that JL was looking a little more concerned than the rest of us. Her hand was resting on the butt of her pistol. She finally relaxed and started to grin. We walked on toward the corrals with people asking Big Mike how it felt to be backed down by an eight-year-old little girl. He took it all in good humor.

In the corral, we had several horses that had been started with our usual method. They knew about being led and having a saddle strapped to their back. We used a big horse to get them to follow behind and accept things. While being led, someone rode them off and on and usually in the river. This kept anyone from getting hurt if they came off the horse and helped the horse figure out it wouldn't be hurt, either. We did this until they calmed down and seemed to be comfortable. There was, however, the first ride. No lead horse, just the rider and the horse. This was a dangerous time and we tried to minimize the risk by not doing it too early, but it was a judgement call.

I had been working with a horse that we all decided was ready for his first ride in the fifty-foot round pen. We used a round pen because the horse can only go so fast in a confined space like that. If they want to run, we just let them. Running in circles soon taught them that they were not going anywhere, and they slowed down. It was then that we started teaching them about responding to the rider. This was all good and well unless the horse broke in two and started to buck. We spent a lot of time trying to avoid that little problem. Yet, that is just what happened to me that day. We all misjudged this horse. He started to buck, and he was good at it. I was hanging in there until a sharp turn had me flying through the air. Problem I had was my foot got hung up in the stirrup. The horse was throwing a fit, and I couldn't get loose. He dragged me halfway around the pen. I thought I was done for when Big Mike jumped off the fence and grabbed the horse's head. He held on, and the horse had no option but to slow down. He finally got the horse stopped and some of the boys rushed out to free up my foot.

When they dragged me away, Big Mike said, "Something in my gut told me this horse was not ready, but I didn't listen to myself. Pull Chris' saddle and strap mine on. We are in now and will have to do this the hard way."

Big Mike held the horse by the head while some of the boys switched saddles. They got it done and backed away. Like a cat, Big Mike sprang up and got his feet in the stirrups. He held the horse's nose to his knee with the lead rope. The horse could only go in tight circles. He would let the horse's head straighten out, and when the horse started to buck, he would pull it back. The horse started to calm down and finally stood quiet, getting air. Big Mike looked at Uncle Dockie.

"Boss, it's real important that we don't quit now. I need to ride Sneaky Pete out for a few hours and make this bad experience a good one."

Uncle Dockie looked toward the gate. "Open it up, boys."

When the gate was open, Sneaky Pete flew out with Big Mike sticking in the saddle. They rode out of sight.

JL said, "That horse had me fooled. I think Big Mike had me fooled also."

We went back to work and things went like we thought they would. Two hours later, Big Mike and Sneaky came riding up. Horse was quiet; soaking wet, but calm.

C-Bar

Uncle Dockie asked, "What you think about this horse, Big Mike?"

"He'll make a good horse, but what we do with him now will decide if he is cold-backed or not."

A cold-backed horse is one that seems fine until you get in the saddle the first time each day. They will cut loose and buck for a while until they decide to give up. Some horses will do this all their lives. Seems to be a habit they don't get over. It's just something you don't look forward to every day and then you tend to avoid the horse. This just makes horse's bad habit even worse.

Big Mike said, "Boss, I need to ride ol' Sneaky every day for a week. He must not be allowed to get this started."

"I agree with you, Mike. He's yours until you think he's over it."

The next day, Mike climbed on and Sneaky Pete bucked. Mike made that behavior a bad idea. He rode the horse hard. On the second day, he did the same and so did Mike. On the third day, Sneaky Pete gave up the bucking and never did it again. Big Mike had proven himself not to be a brute but a good horseman, and this is what a good puncher is about. A good horseman has the respect of everyone. Mike had found a home with the C-Bar.

As time went on, Mike became like family. He loved

the kids. On Sunday he would play with them in the river. He threw them up in the air, and they splashed in the water. This was endless fun for them all. JL's son was much younger. Mike would not throw him as high as the older kids. With that he proved to us he had something called judgement, and that is a good quality.

Mike and Aunt Marsha became close. They would sit on the porch, snap green beans and visit. She mothered on him like she did everyone else, and he loved it. He was also learning to read with Uncle Dockie. The interesting relationship was he and Winston, JL's husband. These two were as different as night and day. Winston was refined English royalty, and Big Mike the rough-sawn product of the West. Big Mike would study Winston and seemed to appreciate his ways. Winston taught him to play chess, and Mike eventually became a good game for Winston. There is an old saying: Rough colts make good horses. Mike proved there was some truth in this old proverb.

I was fixing fences with Mike one day and I asked him, "Mike, do you like it here on the C-Bar?"

"Chris, I have found something here that I didn't even know existed. I found peace and contentment. I hope I never have to leave."

I responded, "I know exactly what you mean, Mike. Like you, this is all I need in the world."

I'm going to skip years ahead now and tell you about

C-Bar

Big Mike and the C-Bar. I will then bring you back to the story as it happened.

Mike was one of the best hands we ever had. A hard-working and loyal man. We had many adventures and saved each other's life more than once. The time came that he was losing weight and slowing down. After a while, we all knew that he was dying. It was heartbreaking to see this mountain of a man waste away. I spent a lot of time looking after him.

He whispered to me, "Chris, take me outside. I don't want to die inside. I want to feel the sun on my face." I picked him up and walked down to the river. We sat on the bank with our feet in the water. He laid his head on my chest and passed away. I cried like a baby.

Big Mike Callahan, one bad sum bitch.

Big Mike and I were in a line camp one night, sitting around the stove. I asked him to tell me about his life. What follows is exactly what he told me. That was one of the best evenings I've ever spent. I hope you appreciate it as much as I did.

***

My name is Big Mike Callahan. I have been in dozens of bar fights and only been whipped once. That story is coming. I stand six-foot-six. Weigh in at 250 pounds. On top of that I'm quick and agile as a cat. Lighting fast. The two things I like most in this world is whores and fighting. If I had to choose, I'd pick fighting first. Jumping on a whore is one thing, but throwing a man across the room is a lot more fun. I have a fighting secret. I don't try to punch or kick. All I do is grab and throw them against something hard. You know, like a wall, a table, a bar or even the floor. Why should I bust up my hands when I don't have to?

I was born on a ranch in Kansas. My pa was big and mean, and my ma even bigger and meaner. I learned early what respect is. When we went to town, everyone stepped aside or tried to be friendly. People seemed to kiss our asses and we liked it. Never saw people try to haggle with my pa over anything. He said a price he wanted to get or pay, and people agreed real quick. I never saw him buy a drink. When he came in the saloon, the first drink was always on the house and people around him started lining drinks up on the bar. He was right popular.

Every now and then, a drunk stranger would try to back him down. This was great fun. The crowd would try to figure where the drunk was going to land and make room for the crash. One time I saw two young bucks try him. He picked them both up and slapped them together like a couple of rugs. Then he walked outside and threw them both down on the street. They didn't even move after that. The saloon crowd loved that, and the drinks piled up. The bartender thanked him for taking out the trash.

My ma was even more terrifying. She stood well over six-foot. When she was not happy, I'm telling you, nobody for a mile around was happy. She struck terror in my heart, and I never saw Pa go up against her, either. Let me tell you the truth about something—if someone can strike fear in me and Pa, that person is as bad as it gets.

Growing up weren't easy, but I learned to take a beating and live through it. How I look at it is great training. When I got to my teen years, I had my full growth and loved to fight. My ma and pa had the bluff on me, though, and I didn't ever try to sass them. I truly loved them two mean bastards. I smile just thinking about them.

Working on a ranch weren't no real hardship. Only problem I ever had was finding a horse big and tough enough to carry me all day. Sometimes people would give me a horse that they couldn't do anything with and was glad to be rid of. Hell, I enjoyed the battle. Some horses are downright mean and tough, and this provided a lot of fun. Truth is they made great working horses when they decided to give up being the boss.

During the branding season, I was always the one on the ground. Someone would rope and drag the steer to the fire. It was up to me to wrassel them to the ground for the hot iron to be put on their hide. Great fun.

But there are some things even I won't tangle with. Civilized fighting is one thing, but there are those thugs who don't play nice. Let me tell you about them—usually quiet, no big mouth, most are on the small side. When they look at you, they show no fear. The reason is because they carry a Colt, and Sam Colt equalized every man. Hell, most men carry a gun, but most won't use it. It's just a fashion statement. However, some will and those are the ones to figure out quick.

I learned this the hard way. My pa and I were in a saloon drinking. Pa had too much to drink and got in a fighting mood. There was a table of men playing poker and minding their own business. Pa threw a glass of beer at them, and it crashed on the poker table, making a big mess. All but one got up and left the table. He was just like the ones I described earlier.

He said, "Mister, I don't like rudeness. You need to apologize."

Pa walked over to the table. "You scrawny little shit, what are you going to do about it?"

Cold as ice, the man said, "End the world as you know it."

Pa reached for him, and lighting fast, the man pulled a Colt and shot Pa through the heart. Big strong and mean didn't help even a little bit. Pa was dead. The law said it was self-defense. About a week later, Ma went for him, and he shot her dead just as quick. The man left town. Sheriff said his name was John Wesley Harden. I never saw him again, and truth is I never looked real hard. The town really couldn't have cared less. I think they were glad to be rid of us.

Without Ma and Pa, I gave up the ranch. Sold out and went traveling. Seemed like every saloon I walked into, my size drew attention. Always a tough guy wanting to be a big shot and whip me. Of course, it never happened.

One day I had a big idea. My test was successful. I walked into a saloon and announced to everyone that I could whip any and all comers, and I was willing to put my money where my mouth was. The locals didn't know me, but every town has a favorite tough guy, so bets were always easy to find and word would go out with the challenge. The local big dog would show up soon to protect his reputation. I liked small places to fight in because I could grab them easier. A saloon was always perfect. Pretty soon their man would walk in and the room went quiet. I was pointed out and on he came. The bets were made and then came the evil eye thing for a few seconds, one trying to size up the other.

I always waited for them to throw the first punch. This brought their body to me. I would duck the punch and grab hold. I always knew where they would fall so I just did my thing and slammed them against something. The first throw usually didn't do them in, but they were always slowed up a lot, so I grabbed them again and picked another hard place for them to land. This really softened them up, and the third slam was usually just for fun.

I collected my bets, drank all the free beer and I was now the local hero. Sometimes I could even get a second local victim but could never get the good betting odds, so I would then need to move on.

As time went on, I figured out that the bigger towns were a good way to go. They all had a lot of saloons. I could start on one end of town and in a few days make a lot of money before the word got around about me. Some of the cow towns were good places to work also. There was always a new bunch of cowboys coming to town with someone they thought could whip me. For me, this was an easy way to make a good living. Whup the local tough, get treated like a big shot, drink for nothing and when the money ran out it was off to another saloon.

I found another way to extend my work without having to move on as often. After my reputation got around, I would announce that I could whip any two locals. This just started it all over again. I had to work a little harder, but I found new tricks. I didn't wait for them to throw the first punch. I jumped quick, grabbed one and threw him against the other. Now they were both down and couldn't come at me the same time. From that point, it was just the same old thing. I even learned more tricks. After my reputation spread, I would just wait for the word to get around outside of town. There was always a corn cob who came to town, thinking he could take me on. I almost felt sorry for them. They were strong and all, but the town people have a lot more practice fighting. I guess you could say I was developing my trade.

Little slant-eyed son of a bitch

I was way down south in some shit town, you know where the hoot owls fuck the chickens. I ran my mouth just like always when a man answered my challenge. Not a big man. In fact, a little slant-eyed fella who maybe weighed 150 pounds. When he came in, I thought it was a joke, and I laughed out loud. Hell, I could throw him over the building! But it wasn't a joke.

He walked up to me and said, "Mr. Mike, my people are poor and need money. I am willing to bet all we have—five hundred dollars. What odds you give me?"

I responded, "Hell, I don't care. What odds you want?"

He responded, "Can you do 5 to 1?"

I said, "Hell, I don't care. If that's what you want."

"Mr. Mike, can you pay when you lose?"

"Well, little fella, I don't have twenty-five hundred dollars. But it don't matter. I ain't going to lose."

"Sorry, Mr. Mike, you must have money."

The crowd was wanting to see the show, so several people came forward, taking the odds, and the ball was open. He stood there in a funny way, just waiting for me to make a move. I got tired of this silliness and grabbed for him. Problem was that he deflected my hands and stepped aside, and then the little bastard kicked me when I went by. That really pissed me off. I was going for him, but he wasn't fighting fair. Slippery little slant-eyed son of a bitch. This went on for at least ten minutes.

Next thing I know, we were outside in the street and I couldn't corner him. The crowd was gathering and having a good time, watching me look stupid. Another ten minutes, and I was gettin' tired. Problem for me was he looked just fine. Wasn't even breathing hard. Every time I reached for him, I missed and got kicked for my effort, and let me tell you, it was beginning to hurt.

Another ten minutes, and I was moving like I was an old man. The crowd was now cheering for him and telling him to put me away. So he did just that. I was standing there with my hands down, panting like a dog, when he did a spin and kicked me in the head. Down I went, and all I could do was crawl away. The crowd loved him and couldn't care less about me. It was a bad day.

With my reputation in the gutter, I decided to leave town for a better business climate. You know, somewhere that I wasn't known. I ended up in Prescott, Arizona Territory. Prescott was a well-to-do town. Lots of gold mining and ranching going on. Money was

C-Bar

flowing. First night there, I spent the night with a whore who robbed me blind. Woke up with a hangover and broke. Now that's was big problem for me. I needed working capital for my line of work. I could find a fight easy enough, but if I didn't have money to bet on myself, only one option left—get a job. Build up funds and return to what worked for me.

Asking around, all I could find was ranch work. Man by the name of Dockie Barnett at the C-Bar Ranch needed help so I hired on. Remember me telling you about the type of man who was dangerous? Quiet, cold-eyed, no fear and carries a gun? That was him. I knew he would kill me in a heartbeat, so I gave him respect. I was living in the bunk house and things seemed to be going pretty good.

Problem I had was another cow puncher named Chris Babb. Just the kind of person I don't like. He really didn't say or do anything wrong, I just didn't like him. Other people liked him. Friendly but not a fighter. The kind of man that wants to talk about problems, not kick ass and get them over with quick. Makes me think of a city slicker. I put up with him for a while, but then one day I was just in a bad mood. I walked into the cook shack, and he was already there eating. I reached down, grabbed his shirt, and threw him on the floor. Then I started eating his food. This should have started a fight, but it didn't.

"You're in my seat, city boy."

He just got up and got more food and sat down across the table.

"City boy, can't you see I need more eggs?"

He got up and brought me more eggs. Just what I thought he was—yellow. He then left the cook shack. I finished eating and stepped out the door when a blinding flash hit me in the face. I went down hard. I found out later he hit me with a chunk of firewood. I guess fighting fair never occurred to him. He then tied my feet and got his horse. Dallied off and dragged me down to the river, across and back again. I was close to dead by that time. I can remember people talking.

Dockie said, "What he do, Chris?"

His daughter said, "He pushed Chris, Pa, and got what he deserved."

Dockie got down in my ear. "You're lucky Chris is a nice guy. I would have killed you." He stuck some money in my pocket and told them to haul me into Prescott to the doc. Dockie got close to me again. "Big Mike, when you heal up, leave town and don't come back. Do you understand?"

All I could do was nod my head. A bunch of them threw me in a buckboard and off I went. I spent two weeks with the doc before I could get around. I needed to go somewhere, so I took the first ride out of town I could find. It was going to Stanton, a mining town south of Prescott. I hobbled into the Stanton saloon and spent a few days. Come to find out, Charlie Stanton owned the place.

He sat down at my table, saying, "Boy, you look a little on the down-and-out side of things."

"Truth is, Mr. Stanton, you are right."

He was curious. "What happened?"

"I got crossways of the crew on the C-Bar Ranch."

He nodded his head as if he understood. "I know Dockie Barnett. Don't like the man. He and I almost came to violence. Let me make you an offer."

"I'm in no position to turn down any offer, Mr. Stanton. What you have on your mind?"

"You can stay with me until you get healed up. I have a bunkhouse for you to stay in and three meals a day. When you can, you go to work for me to square up."

Since I had very few options, my response was, "I'm your man."

Working for Charlie Stanton

Charlie turned out being a pretty good fella for me. When I was able, he hired me as a bouncer and liked my enforcement abilities. On one occasion, he asked me to do something that was hard but I did it.

"Mike, I have a problem with a man named Barney Martin. I need you to burn down his barn."

I've done worse, so I agreed. The man rebuilt it, so Charlie sent me out to burn it again. Then it was Barney's house that needed burning. He sent me out to put the fear in people now and then. Just the kind of work I'm good at. We got along like old friends. He came to me again with an order. I went along thinking I might be able to do it.

"Mike, this Martin fella ain't scaring easy. He needs to be done away with. He is taking his family to Phoenix. I need them all to disappear."

I went along with the people Charlie sent to do this, but I just couldn't take part in it. Damn if they didn't kill the whole family, then burned them up in their wagon. I found out that there were some things even I couldn't do.

Two weeks later, I was out doing an errand for Charlie when Chris Babb walked into the bar with a shotgun. "You Charlie Stanton?"

Charlie nodded his head. Babb let loose with both barrels. Killed ol' Charlie dead, and I was unemployed again. I swore right then and there I would kill Chris

Babb when I got the chance. My life just kept going downhill when he got involved.

I wandered around for a year or so, back to my old tricks. Made a good living and enjoyed my celebrity. Never had to venture to the far side of the law again, just beat people up and collected money. I was working my way around Arizona, town to town. Every town the same. Fighting, making money and blowing it on whores and whiskey. A damn fine life.

Tombstone

I liked mining towns. Lot of money and miners getting drunk, thinking they were tough. Just my kind of place. Tombstone was being talked about, so I wandered that way. Walked into a saloon called Freddy's Place. Nice joint. I was just about to yell out my challenge when I looked around the room, and who do I see playing poker? None else than Chris Babb. I finally had him away from the C-Bar.

So I walked over and said, "Well, well, Chris Babb. I hear they call you the Chicago Kid now. I've been wanting to break you in two, and now I finally get the chance."

He replied, "Well, if it ain't Big Mike. Been swimming lately?"

I was pissed. I started for him when the table broke into laughter. A man jumped up and hit me on the head with his pistol. Down I went, out cold. I woke up the next day in a jail cell. Jailer tells me I must be the dumbest man walking. I picked a fight with the Earp clan and Doc Holiday. Chris Babb was their friend. Hell, I didn't know! Fella what owns the saloon I was in when I had my misfortune came to talk with me. Wanted to know about the Chicago Kid. I told him what I knew, he gave me a hundred dollar bill and left. Next day, I was escorted to the stage line and put aboard with instructions:

"Don't come back."

That really set me back. Almost broke and needing to heal up again. I found work in a mine just north of Tucson. I truly hated that job. Hard labor and dangerous dirty work. They liked me because I could shovel more ore than most, so they paid me well, but as soon as I had a stake and healed up, it was back to work in my chosen trade. For some reason, all I could think about was getting even with Babb. He haunted me night and day. The one man who hurt me the most and seemed the easiest to crush, but I just couldn't get it done. Was he lucky or smart? Hell, I didn't know, but I decided to go back to Prescott and call him out in a fair fight.

Prescott

When I got to Prescott, I needed some money. I thought I would get a little work done so out my challenge went:

"I am the toughest man you have ever seen and I can whip anyone in this shithole town. Bring him on and bring your money. I'm taking bets."

My old plan didn't work this time. Whiskey Row just weren't big enough to avoid attention. The sheriff found me real quick. Probably because he was sitting in the saloon at a table playing poker when I made my announcement.

He stood up and walked over to me. "Boy, if you think you can start trouble here, you are wrong. Me and three more will have you in jail before you can get wound up. Do you understand?"

I knew better than to push the law, so I backed down. "Yes, sir. I understand. No trouble here."

Prescott was a bust and I was almost broke. Next day I was sitting at a table, brooding, when I heard the name Chris Babb come up. I asked around and found out he had returned to Prescott. I spread the word that I wanted Chris Babb to face me in a fair fight. The word started circulating. Then later the next day, in walked the Barnett family, which included Babb. Babb walked over to my table. The rest of them stayed at the bar, all looking real hard at me. He sat down and laid his shotgun on the table. We just looked at each other for a few seconds.

I started, "Well, well, if it ain't the Chicago Kid. You must have heard that I wanted another go at you.

Problem for you is that I'm ready this time. Are you prepared for me to break your back?"

Chris spoke, and I must say he didn't have any fear in his voice.

"Big Mike, you don't kill easy. I am impressed. Here is what happens today—no matter if I live or die, my family will kill you. They know better than to let you live and then have to look over their shoulders, waiting for you to show up again. This will end today. Maybe for both of us. Big Mike, I don't want to fight you. I would be a fool to want to. I have a little girl to think about. Things have changed for me. However, I can be your best friend or your worst enemy. I would rather be your friend. You're a big, mean son of a bitch, and having you for an enemy is not a smart thing to make happen. So, what's it going to be, Big Mike? Are we friends, or do we both die today?"

I had to think for a while. He was right. To die over an old score don't make sense. For some reason I still don't understand, my anger was gone. All I felt was relief. I was overwhelmed with envy. This man had a family willing to let him fight me and all ready to kill me if he lost. I think Chris Babb had gotten to me in some way.

I looked around the room and said in a quiet way so no-one heard me, "Just how do we get out of this problem and not lose respect from everyone watching?"

Babb then reached out his hand to me. He didn't care one whit about losing the respect of those watching. He let me off the hook at his expense. I reached out, and we shook hands.

He stood up and said loud enough for everyone to hear, "Big Mike, you are known far and wide for being a good hand. Would you like to work on the C-Bar again?"

This was a big surprise for me. Truth is I was kind of got by the offer. After all this, he was willing to start over.

"Well, Chicago Kid, I need a job real bad. I would come back to the C-Bar under one condition."

He responded, "What is that condition?"

"That you don't hit me with a chunk of firewood again or make me take a bath in the river."

We both laughed, and the crowd watching was wide-eyed. We shook hands again.

"Condition accepted."

"Now I have a condition," said Chris.

I responded, "What is that?"

"That I don't have to serve you breakfast in the mornings."

We both laughed again. I said, "Condition accepted."

"Come out tomorrow and start work. You know our routine."

"I'll be there about sunrise," I told him.

Babb turned and walked out. Right behind him was his family. The room came back to life. I was sitting there pondering it all when a man walked over to me.

"I guess you showed the Chicago Kid for what he really is. Good work. I never liked the son of a bitch."

To this day, I don't know why I did what I did just then, but I grabbed the loud mouth and threw him across the room.

I then said, "Listen up, everyone, nobody speaks bad about my friends."

***

So that was the story just as Big Mike told it to me. Let's get back to where we left off...

Chapter 5
The Ranch to the East

Taking Eric Alan's advice, we had stashed our gold and waited for an opportunity. It came. A man named Russell Jones rode up to the house. Uncle Dockie and Little Dez were sitting on the porch, reading. As usual, he approached the house but didn't dismount until asked.

Uncle Dockie looked up. "Hello, Russell. Get down and rest awhile. Do you want anything to drink?"

"Thanks, Dockie."

He dismounted and dropped his reins to the ground. The horse was trained to stay put. He walked up on the porch and sat down on a chair.

"How is Miss Marsha and the kids? All well, I hope."

"Russell, we are all well, and how about you?"

"Well, Dockie, some things have changed for me. I have inherited a farm back in Iowa. It's too good to let go, so I am going back East. I want to sell my ranch. Are you interested?"

Little Dez jumped up and ran into the house. Uncle Dockie responded, "Just might be, Russell. What you have in mind?"

Aunt Marsha came out with Little Dez. She sat down and Dez raced away. "Well, look who came to see us? How are you, Russell?"

Strange thing was how gabby Aunt Marsha was. She talked about the weather and all sorts of things that no one really had any interest in. This dragged on for ten minutes or so when Eric Alan walked up.

"Hello, Mr. Jones," he said. "How are you today?"

Aunt Marsha stood up and Eric Alan took her seat. She looked at Uncle Dockie. "Dockie, I need you to help me for a minute. Would you come inside?"

Since no-one can tell her no, Uncle Dockie got up and followed Aunt Marsha in the house. This left Russell and Eric Alan on the porch.

"So, Mr. Jones, what brings you here to see us?"

Mr. Jones looked confused. "Who am I supposed to talk business with, young man?"

"Pa has given this part of the ranch business up to me. I speak for all of us. What you have in mind?"

He repeated what he told Uncle Dockie. Eric Alan responded, "Well, Mr. Jones, we are like everyone else and strapped for cash, but just what do you have in mind?"

Mr. Jones sat back in his chair. "I have six sections. River runs down the middle. That is three miles of river. And you know as well as I do that water is gold in this part of the world. I have four hundred head of cattle. The ranch house and corrals are all in good shape. Are you interested?"

Eric Alan wrinkled up his forehead and looked very concerned. "I guess we could be. What kind of money you askin'?"

"Ten thousand dollars, and that's a steal."

Eric Alan flinched as if he were shot. "That is a powerful lot of cash. What kind of time frame do you have?"

This is where Mr. Jones went wrong. He told the truth. "Just as fast as I can. First one with the money gets it, and I'm gone."

Eric Alan never let on that this is what he needed to hear. "Mr. Jones, we will come tomorrow, and you can show us around. Maybe we can work something out."

Mr. Jones left Eric Alan sitting on the porch. Uncle Dockie returned.

"Did Russell talk with you about selling out? I wanted to be here, but your ma had me doing errands."

"We talked about it, Pa. I'm going over there

tomorrow to look things over."

Uncle Dockie looked confused. "What is he asking?"

"He wants ten thousand, but he ain't getting that much."

"Seems to me, Eric Alan, that is a fair number."

"Maybe so, Pa, but he ain't getting that much."

Before Uncle Dockie could say another word, Eric Alan was up and gone. The next day, Eric Alan, Big Mike and I were riding to the Jones ranch. It looked pretty much like our ranch. Good water, grass and trees. We arrived at the ranch house about mid-morning and were greeted by Mr. Jones.

"Well, boys, what you want to see first?"

Eric Alan said, "Cattle and boundaries. Cattle first."

We rode the rest of the day, looking over the herd. Typical mix of range stock. The cattle count came up with the same number as Jones did. Four hundred head, give or take a few. There were also twenty-five ranch horses. That night we inspected the ranch house and found it in good repair. He was a single man so we all slept in the main house. The next day was spent riding the fence line. It was all in good shape. The three of us had a huddle and the conversation went like this:

Eric Alan said, "What do you think, boys?"

I had this to say: "Seems like we can't go wrong if we get this at a good price. Remember our motto—we ain't buying it if we ain't stealing it. That is good business."

We both looked at Big Mike. "Seems to me if we were to buy the ranch for what we could sell the cattle and horses for, it's as good as free. We can always restock over time."

Eric Alan had the look of confidence on his face. "Let's see what we can do."

When negotiating, there is one rule—everyone is lying. I was betting Jones was as much or more then we were. So we sat at the table that evening and got started.

Mr. Jones began, "So, are you interested?"

Eric Alan had a look of worry on his face. "Mr. Jones, we would love to own this ranch. Here is the problem. You want cash and you want it quick. That puts us at a big disadvantage. We almost went broke borrowing from the bank, and we won't do that again. So here is what I can offer you—we have thirty-five hundred in gold, and that is what we can afford."

Mr. Jones immediately went into a big, loud 'No.' "Boys, that is highway robbery! I would have to be out of my mind to do that."

Big Mike looked at Eric Alan and said, "Eric Alan, I have five hundred saved away, and you can have that if you need it." This was an absolute lie, but Big Mike knew how to play this game.

Mr. Jones again started his protest. "Four thousand dollars is not even going to happen. I'll turn the stock loose and burn the house before I do that."

Then it was my turn. "Eric Alan, I have a thousand I can throw in, but that is every penny I have in the world."

Eric Alan was looking at the floor then he looked up real slowly. "Mr. Jones, we can't give you any more then we have. It's five thousand, or we can't make the deal happen."

Jones sat back in his chair with a sigh. "You assholes have a deal. When can we close?"

"Mr. Jones, I was a lawyer in Chicago. I can see to all the paperwork. Is that good for you?"

"I guess it has to be. What do we need to do?"

"I need to ask you a question—do you owe any money on the place?"

A big frown crossed his face. "I ain't never owed anybody for anything. Especially no bank."

Another rule was making sure you were not being lied to. "Then you don't mind if I go to town and check with the recorder's office?"

He responded, "Don't mind one bit."

"Then I will go to Prescott tomorrow and get all the paperwork created. Let's draw up a contract and seal the deal. We can meet back here in three days to finalize."

We drew up our preliminary deal and signed it. The next morning, I did a long trot to Prescott while Eric Alan and Big Mike went back home. Two days later, I returned to the Jones ranch just a little bit ahead of Eric Alan. I was waiting on the trail when he rode up. There was Eric Alan, Big Mike, JL and, much to my disappointment, Uncle Dockie. I had to speak up.

"Uncle Dockie, we have made the deal and will sign all the papers, but I have a concern."

JL jumped in real fast. "Don't worry, Chris. We have been lecturing Pa all the way here to keep quiet and let us get this deal finished."

I looked over at Uncle Dockie.

"Don't worry, Chris. I'll keep quiet. If I soured this deal, my name would be mud at home. Your Aunt Marsha laid down the law to me."

I felt better knowing that Aunt Marsha got involved.

She was the only person in this world that Uncle Dockie really listened to. We all rode in and were met by Mr. Jones. His wagon was packed and he was waiting for us. He looked at me.

"I assume, Chris, that all went well in town?"

"Yes, Mr. Jones, it did. I have all the paperwork, and we can finalize the deal."

Big Mike said, "Boss, why don't we ride around and let me show you some of the layout while they get this boring paperwork taken care of."

JL was quick to join in. "Good idea, Mike. Pa and I are wanting to see what we are spending all our savings on."

Before Uncle Dockie could say a word, they were on both sides of him, crowding him toward the corrals. The rest of us went inside and sat at the table. I got out the paperwork and carefully described what it was all about. Mr. Jones couldn't sign quick enough. He then said, "Where is the money?"

Eric Alan pulled a bag out of his saddlebag. Inside were gold coins in the amount of five thousand dollars. He grabbed it and looked very relieved.

"I'm going to admit something to you boys. I know that a fire sale is when things go cheap. I was prepared to take less. Guess I got over on you with this deal."

What have I been telling you all along—deal making is a liars' contest. I could tell Eric Alan was looking a little unhappy, so I spoke up.

"Well, Mr. Jones, you sure did. We will have to just make the best of this and work hard to make it come out good for us."

We all stood up and walked out with Jones smiling real big. He jumped on his wagon and drove away. About then Uncle Dockie, JL and Mike rode up.

Uncle Dockie said, "I feel kind of bad about this. Feel like we took advantage of him."

Eric Alan responded, "Hell, Pa, he thinks he took us down the river on this deal. Don't feel sorry for him."

JL got in the conversation. "Glad he feels good about it. All I know is that we just made the deal of a lifetime."

We all laughed, dismounted and went inside to rest a while. We had work to do.

Mark Baugher

Chapter 6
The Roundup

After resting and getting something to eat, we started the roundup. Camp Verde was a few miles farther east. There were cattle buyers there. We rode back to our easternmost boundary and started driving all the cattle toward Camp Verde. The roundup was going well. The cattle were not wild, so it was an easy gather. The job took three days and we were holding the cattle outside of town. Eric Alan rode in to find a buyer and check out the prices. He was back a few hours later with a buyer and the haggling started. They rode among the cattle, and Eric Alan was selling his ass off. The buyer was picking them apart, but Eric Alan was telling him how many years it took to build this fine herd. They eventually came to the price of fifteen dollars per head. The buyer had his people run them through a squeeze shoot to make a count. The total was four hundred and twelve head for a total of $6,118.

We settled up and were riding toward home when Uncle Dockie said, "Well, let me get this deal all understood—I rode over to the Jones Ranch with five thousand dollars in gold. Now I'm riding back home with $6,118, plus four thousand acres and three miles of river added to our ranch. It just don't seem possible. Could we go to jail for this kind of thing?"

JL had her response: "Pa, Jones thinks he skinned us. So he's happy. We were the only people standing there with the cash in hand, so the deal was ours for the making. Your dumb butt son pulled the deal together. I may have to think a little bit different about him from now on. It's called good deal making."

Uncle Dockie just looked bewildered. "Maybe I'll just let you young people do all the deals from now on."

JL looked over at us with a big smile and look of relief.

Chapter 7
Pilgrims

One beautiful day, JL and I were out checking on our cattle. JL was being her usual pest and giving me a hard time.

"Well, cuz, maybe you ain't a complete sissy. I'm thinking you are really only half a sissy."

This was typical of her. She knew men didn't like their manhood made fun of and she was quick to use that on Eric Alan and myself. I was fighting back the impulse to tell her how wrong she was, but I held it back. I tried never to give her the satisfaction of knowing she got to me.

"JL, I appreciate you complimenting me like you are. I guess only being a half-sissy is an improvement for me."

She always liked to get me riled but she was not getting it done, so she reached deeper into her bag of tricks. She knew a man's weaknesses and loved to use them.

"I heard some gossip about you."

What the hell… I went along with it. "Oh, you did? Well, just what did you hear?" I knew this was going to be good.

"Some of the local gals got a peek of you swimming in the river."

Again, I went along. "Oh, no!" I feigned horror. "I hope they didn't see me swimming naked!!"

"Yessiree, they did, and they were not impressed with what they saw."

Ol' JL knew us menfolk well. She was a master at torment. I really wanted to defend myself. Hell, everybody knew the river was cold! Ain't none of us menfolk look our best when we jump in cold water. I just bit my tongue and didn't say a word. She could tell I was close to barking at her. You know what she did then? Just smiled and held her hand up in the air with her thumb and first finger about an inch apart. Well, at that point she had me.

"Very funny. You are just very Goddamn funny, you asshole."

She laughed so loud, I was soon joining in. I just wish I knew more about women and had some ammunition to work with, but truth is they are just not bothered with things like this. The have advantages, and that's for sure.

We rode up to a hilltop to get a better view when we saw Eric Alan's horse tied to a tree down by the river. We rode down to see what he was doing. When we found him, he was sound asleep on a red sandstone rock. Boots were off, and his feet were dangling in the water. We dismounted and walked over to him. He opened one eye and looked at us.

"Well, little brother, been working so hard you wore yourself plumb out?"

"No, sis, I ain't done a lick of work all day. Just been lying here, thinking."

JL looked at me and then back at him. "I must say, I am impressed that you are thinking at all. What you thinking about?"

"The meaning of life, sis."

"Whoa, now," she laughed, "that's some deep thinking coming from the likes of you. Figure anything out?"

"Why, yes, I have. I think we were put here to have as much fun as possible."

JL made the face she makes when she's figured something out.

"And by 'fun' do you mean cheap whiskey and easy women?"

Eric Alan looked at JL as if she were completely dumb.

"Hell, yes! What other kind of fun is there? What

about you, JL? Before Winston arrived, you never seemed to have any fun. Have you ever drunk any whiskey?"

JL just shook her head. "Not much."

"And all those men who came around. You never gave them a chance. How come?"

"They were all so dumb I couldn't stand to be around them."

Eric Alan just looked puzzled. "Dumb... What you mean dumb?"

By now, he was sitting up and talking. JL just smiled. "You know, like you," she said. She put her foot on his shoulder and pushed him head over heels into the cold river. He went completely under. When he came up, he was spitting water and mad as a hornet.

"JL, I'm going to kick your ass!"

We knew it was time to make a break, so we ran for our horses. Got mounted up just as he was getting to us on a dead run. Our horses sprinted off and left him behind. JL just couldn't stand it. She turned when at a safe distance and called back, "Better get out of there and get dried off. You might catch a cold."

We loped off, laughing our asses off. When down the trail and at a safe distance, JL turned to me. "Have I ever told you about Eric Alan coming home drunk and going up against Pa?"

I was very surprised to hear this. "He didn't really do that, did he?"

"Believe this or not, he did. I was in the house with Ma, getting ready to eat some pie fresh out of the oven. Eric Alan walked in drunk, put his fingers in the pie and pulled some to his mouth. Pie was all over his face. Very disgusting. Ma slapped his hand. Eric Alan's drunken response was, 'Damn, Ma, it's not a jar of cookies. Why you always gotta treat me like a little kid? I'm a full grow'd up man. If I want a piece of pie, I'm gonna have me a piece of pie.'

"Ma was pissed but kept calm. She said, 'Young man, I think it's in your best interest to show some respect around here.'

"He came right back with, 'Ain't like anyone around here shows me any respect.'

"Of course, I had to chime in. I said, 'Well, little brother, that's because you are a cocky little shithead.'

"Eric Alan was trying to strut his stuff now. He said, 'Well, maybe this cocky little shithead will eat the pie all by himself!'

"Then things got fun. Pa walked in and just stood there behind Eric Alan. Eric Alan turned to him and Pa said real quiet, 'I would wash my face and apologize to these ladies were I you.'

"As soon as Pa said that, I knew he was in trouble. He was drunk and said the wrong thing. He sassed, 'You know what, Pa? Maybe you used to be able to whip my ass and maybe you used to be able to tell me what to do. But now you are just old.'

"*Pow*! Pa hit him and down he went. He lay there, groaning. Pa sat down at the table. Ma, with a big grin, asked him if he wanted a piece of pie. He said he sure would. While we ate, Pa looked down at him and said, 'Hard growing up, ain't it?' We all laughed. Well, everyone except my dumb brother."

I loved these stories. At least JL was off me and onto someone else. "Since you are on a roll, JL, tell me another story," I prompted.

She pondered for a minute.

"Well, let me tell you this one. You probably know that Uncle NoName is a hard drinker and completely devoted to Pa and us. He would fight a bull, but if Ma is upset with him, he folds up quick. Ma had been doing laundry all day. It was a hot and miserable day. She had it all hung up on the clothesline to dry. It was not there five minutes when in rode a drunk Uncle NoName. He got pulled off his horse by the clothesline and down he went, all wrapped up in sheets and underwear. He was yelling and trying to get up, but all he managed to do was roll around in the dirt with Ma's clean wash. At that moment I was truly afraid for Uncle NoName's life. I have never seen Ma that mad. Eric Alan could get her going but nothing like this.

"She grabbed her rug beater and started wailing away on Uncle NoName. That made him yell even louder. Pa came rushing in to see this brawl. I told him, 'Pa, I think Uncle NoName needs your help. Ma may kill him.' Pa waded in, ducking her rug beater, and grabbed her from behind. He picked her up and walked off with her yelling revenge on Uncle NoName. We didn't see Uncle NoName for several weeks after that.

"But we were eating dinner one evening when the door opened and a hat was tossed in on the floor. A few seconds later, Uncle NoName peeked in the door. 'Is it safe to come in here?' he asked.

"I could have told him that a woman don't forget and forgive that easy. Ma walked over to the door and said, 'NoName, get in here and eat, but don't expect any love coming your way.' He crawled in on his hands and knees like a whipped dog. It was too funny not to laugh. Even Ma had to grin over his antics. From then on, he would ask if it was wash day before he would come to the house."

She grinned from ear to ear. I couldn't help but grin right along with her.

We rode on. We were close to home when we heard

the three-shot distress call. The sound was coming from back towards the river, so we ran our horses that way. Eric Alan was heading that way, too, so he sided in beside us. We spotted Uncle Dockie on a hilltop, waving at us. When we got to him, he had the stone face on. I knew something was bad. We rode a little distance when we came upon the scene.

It was obvious that a family of pilgrims was camped at the river. Wagon was on fire, belongings were scattered everywhere. Two men were tied to a tree and all bloody. An older woman was in the grass, half-naked. They were all dead. This took my mind back to Barney Martin down Stanton way. I was close to being sick. All we could do was stand there and stare. Uncle Dockie walked over to the woman and covered her body.

We were all in shock, saying nothing, when a younger woman came around the side of the wagon with a rifle in her hands. She was in a panic and pointing the gun at us. JL started walking slowly her way. Scared hell out of me but, thinking back, another woman would not be treated same as us men. JL got close when the woman turned the gun around and put the barrel in her mouth. She pulled the trigger. Only noise was a click. The gun was not loaded. She dropped the rifle and fell sobbing into JL's arms.

I wish I could erase this memory from my mind. JL held her while us men stayed back. When her fear had turned to grief, we slowly stepped forward. Between us we got her to shade and got some water down her throat. JL just held her and rocked the woman like you would do a child in the middle of the night. Uncle Dockie picked up the rifle and was looking it over.

I walked over to him. "Uncle Dockie, how you figure this?"

He was quiet for a while then he said, "I know the owner of this rifle. The name Snake is carved in the stock."

Eric Alan said, "Who is that, Pa?"

"Your uncles and I ran into the Snakebite Gang a few years ago. We knew we should kill them, but the opportunity wasn't right so we moved on. They are a murderous gang led by a mute named Snakebite. People as bad as they get. They rob, rape and murder all over the Southwest."

After burying the dead, we got the girl on Eric Alan's horse and took her back to the ranch. Aunt Marsha came out to meet us and never said a word. Just took the woman inside and started taking care of her. We were all standing on the porch when Big Mike walked up. I briefly explained what happened. He was quiet.

Then JL said, "Pa, I'm going to kill those sons of bitches."

Uncle Dockie then replied, "Children, the law should

be doing this, but by the time they got organized the gang would be safe in Mexico. It's up to us to hunt them down, but this is just as dangerous as anything we have ever done. We need to be smart."

JL said, "Hell, Pa, the law here is a joke anyway."

Uncle Dockie looked at Big Mike. "You in?"

Without hesitation, Mike said, "Hell, yes. I'll get trail ready." He turned and walked away.

Uncle Dockie asked, "Jessie Lynn, where is Winston?"

"He's in town and not due back for several days."

Uncle Dockie said, "Well, let's see. There are at least eight or nine of them and only four of us. Let's stop and pick up Bobby and NoName. Bobby is a good man in a fight, and NoName is if he's sober. Everyone gear up and let's be ready in an hour."

We scattered and got ready.

Chapter 8
The Hunt

An hour later, we were lined up and ready. Looked like we were going to war. Everyone had pistols, rifles and shotguns. Saddlebags were bulging with ammunition. We had a packhorse with provisions.

Big Mike said, "I ain't never been fighting with you before, but I play by one rule. There ain't no rules. If I can I shoot them in the back, I will."

Uncle Dockie responded, "I'm glad you are with us, Big Mike. That is just how we work. The animals we are hunting would do the same to us if they could."

We moved out to the burned wagon to pick up their trail. When we got there, JL had a dog ready to track. He sniffed around and then walked off, going south. We followed. Two hours later, we left the trail toward Bobby's cabin. He's one of Uncle Dockie's old friends. They have childhood history. Devoted to each other like brothers. When we rolled up, no-one dismounted. Everyone just stayed horseback and waited. Wasn't long before Bobby came out, ready to go to war. Never a word was said. He just climbed on his horse and rode off with us. Never even asked where we were going. Bobby knew it didn't matter. He was with Dockie no matter what came. I'm sure Uncle Dockie would have been the same were it reversed.

Again we went back to the trail and continued south.

Uncle Dockie pulled up and turned to us.

"NoName lives over that way yonder. Let's swing over and get him."

An hour later, we were lined up in front of a run-down cabin. Looked like hell. We just sat patiently. Wasn't long before a shotgun barrel poked out a hole in the wall.

"I don't know who you sons of bitches are, but I got a shotgun on your ass!!"

JL called out, "Uncle NoName, it's me."

From inside the cabin came, "Jessie Lynn, is that you?"

"Yeah, it's me, Uncle NoName."

We could hear crashing and banging inside, but finally the door opened. Uncle NoName was drunk as a skunk. He leaned against the door frame.

"Well, Jessie Lynn, sweetheart. If I had know'd it was you, I wouldn't have pointed that shotgun in your direction."

He stumbled over to JL and hugged on her leg. He looked at Uncle Dockie.

"What we gonna do, Dockie? Go rob a bank?"

Uncle Dockie just shook his head. "Get on your horse, dipshit. We need help."

NoName replied, "I never did like you, you pile of horse dung." He then looked back at JL. "Jessie Lynn, you are as pretty as your ma. You can't be related to him."

Uncle Bobby just sat there, not saying a word, when NoName looked his way and said, "And you, you ugly bastard, you sure ain't getting any prettier."

About then Eric Alan had NoName's horse and led the fine animal toward us. She was a broken-down nag. Had to be twenty-five years old. The horse was saddled with an old Civil War saddle, worn out and worthless.

NoName walked over to Eric Alan and said, "Damn, boy, you ain't as dumb as you look. Get me up on that horse."

Eric Alan just grinned. NoName hugged on him some and started to play rough when Eric Alan cried out, "Pa, I'm about to kick Uncle NoName's ass!"

The look on NoName's face went hard. "No, he ain't. Help me on that horse, boy. "

Eric Alan had one more thing to say. "You sure you can climb up there? It ain't a one-legged whore."

"Shut up, boy, and help me get up there."

Things were amusing up to now, but it got better. Eric Alan would lift him up and over he would go, landing flat on his back. This happened twice until they got on both sides of his horse and kept him from falling as we rode away. He was a mess and feeling bad. It was not a good day to be Uncle NoName.

Chapter 9
Bobby Finds Out What Is Going On

That night, around the campfire, Uncle Dockie and NoName were sound asleep. The rest of us were just sitting and not able to sleep.

JL commented, "Pa sure is grumpy."

"Sure is. Wonder what's wrong with the old fart?" said Eric Alan.

Bobby sat up. "Is someone going to tell me what we are doing out here?"

Up until now, he had not asked. Been me, I would have wanted to know from the start.

JL explained, "Snakebite and his gang killed a family of pilgrims over by us. Horrible what they did to them."

Eric Alan added, "All but a girl. She ain't in good shape after what they done to her, though."

Bobby got quiet and then said, "Hmm. I can tell you why your pa is in a bad mood. The people we are chasing are a bad lot. We know them."

Eric Alan asked, "How the hell you know them?"

"We ran into them a few years ago. Knew then that we should kill them, but we didn't."

"Why not?" asked JL.

"That's what comes of being civilized. That's your ma's fault."

"The old days. 'Bout time you told us about the old days," said Eric Alan.

Bobby slowly looked at Eric Alan. "Your pa will tell you when he's ready."

"All I know is that I got a lot of uncles I ain't related to. I'm dying to hear those old stories. What the hell were you up to in those good old days?"

Bobby took a minute, but did eventually respond, "The good old days sound a lot better than they were. There's a few things you kids don't know. We survived, but things were hard, real hard. We banded together just to stay alive. One more thing—you don't seem to understand what we are doing. People are gonna die. I just hope it ain't us." With that, Bobby lay back down.

Eric kept talking, "All I know is that I'm finally going to have a story of my own."

"Go to sleep, boy," was Bobby's response.

Chapter 10
The Snakebite Gang

In telling you this story, you are hearing what I witnessed firsthand. There is a more that I did not see. For that I went to Uncle Dockie, Aunt Marcia and JL. They were all willing to fill me in. However, there is the inside tale of the Snakebite Gang that I did not have until later, which was a year after the adventure.

I was eating in a cafe in Prescott one fine day when the sheriff walked in and sat down. He looked around and saw me. He walked over.

"Chris, I have some news you may be interested in hearing."

"Sit down, Sheriff, and fill me in. If you're hungry, I'm buying."

"Thanks, Chris, but I already ate. Have you heard about a man we have in jail called Red River John?"

I was starting to get real curious. "No, I have not," I replied.

"As crazy a man as I ever saw. We caught him about a month ago. Wanted man. He's going to Yuma for life next week. Says he is the last surviving member of the Snakebite Gang."

This took me by surprise because I didn't think there

were any survivors.

"Sheriff, can I speak with the man?"

"Sure, Chris. When you're done, come on over to the jail."

"I'm done."

I stood up and waved Stormin' Norma over. "Norma your food was great as always, but I need to go. No reflection on your grub."

Norma just patted me on the back as I walked out. The sheriff and I walked across Montezuma Street to the court house. The jail was in the basement and the sheriff led me down to that area. God, I hated these kinds of places. The smell was overpowering. It was dark and humid. Full of rats and bugs. The cells were small. Bad place to be.

The sheriff stopped in front of a cell, saying, "John, you have a visitor."

John looked like the outlaw he was. Unkept with desperate eyes. Maybe thirty years old. He responded, "Who the hell wants to see me?"

I stepped closer. "I do. My name is Chris Babb. I'm from the C-Bar."

John didn't respond for a few seconds. He squinted

his eyes at me and asked, "What you want?"

"Just want to ask you some questions."

John responded, "I can do that, but not here. I only answer questions in the sunlit. Where the Lord can see me."

I looked at the sheriff.

He pondered a moment, then said, "Well, Chris, we can do that. I will put shackles on him and escort him outside. He won't go anywhere. There will be a guard watching. Go on out to the south side of the court house. We will bring him out."

I left the cells and was relieved to be outside again. A guard followed soon, leading John out and down the steps. He had on leg irons and wrist cuffs. The guard brought him over to me. John and I sat down on a bench. He sat there for a minute or so soaking up the sun. I didn't push him.

He then slowly looked over at me and said, "So, what you want to know?"

"Were you a member of the Snakebite Gang?"

"Sure enough. If you want to know more, you have to hear my story. I'm going to drag this out if I can. The Lord likes me being in the sunshine."

I thought about things for a few seconds. I decided to let him talk. The more he talked, the more truth I would get out of him.

"That's fine with me. Let me hear your story."

"I was born in West Texas. Orphaned early. Don't even have a real name. Someone called me John, so I took it. It eventually turned into Red River John. Don't know where the Red River part came from. Ain't never even seen that river. I was outlawed early. I figured out how to survive. I took what I needed. Ran with people that were not church-goers. Was on the run from those damned Texas Rangers. I hate those blood sucking assholes.

"One day I stole some cattle from John Slaughter. The old bastard caught me. Was going to hang me, but for some reason didn't do it. Hired me instead. He was putting together a drive and needed help. When I got to know the crew, it was plain to see they were all no better than me. We spent a lot of time gathering up cattle for a drive to Arizona Territory. Funny thing was we weren't real concerned just what brand was on the cattle we gathered. Well, anyway, we got them all to Arizona for ol' John. Most of us quit about that time and went to Tombstone."

I interrupted him at this point. "Did you know Curley Bill and his crowd?"

"Well, hell, yes, I knew him. Him, Johnny Ringo and

all the rest."

"Why didn't you go with them?"

"I ran into a man called John Doe. Now there is one crazy son of a bitch and I love him. Some call him insane. But that don't make him stupid. He was the thinker in the bunch and he put together some good deals. He had us doing raids out into Arizona. We stole women, children and horses. They all had a good market in Mexico. We would go out and come back with enough money to stay drunk for a month. Spent most of our time in Naco, Mexico, just across the border. We owned that town. Rosa's cantina was our hangout."

I interrupted again, "Tell me about Snakebite."

He laughed over that question. "He was John Doe's son. A mute. Never heard him say a word. Cold blooded bastard. I saw him shoot a child for whimpering. Nobody crossed him. He always led our raids out and back."

"Well, John, tell me about the raid you were on that took you up towards Prescott."

"Just like all the rest. Robbin' and killin'."

I asked, "Do you remember a family camped by the river? Two men and two women."

"Sure do. We found them sleeping and tied the men

to a fence. Made them watch while we used their women. Not me, though; the Lord don't take kindly to that sort of thing, and I am a God-fearing man. Yup, Snakebite made them watch and then killed the men with a rock. The older woman came at him, so he killed her too. The younger woman grabbed a rifle and ran into the brush. We didn't have the time to look for her, so we left."

"Do you remember a camp with only one woman?"

"That was a quick in-and-out thing. Killed her because we didn't have no way to take her back to Mexico. Stole what we could carry and burned the wagon. Whole thing was over in five minutes."

"How about a cabin of miners?"

"We came onto a cabin late in the evening. I pounded on the door. Someone made the mistake of coming to see who was out there. He opened the door and got a load of buckshot for his stupidity. Snakebite hauled out the other miner and shot him in the back. We settled in and got comfortable. Later that night, two of our gang were whispering back and forth. One of them was talking about leaving the gang. He thought Snakebite was mute and deaf. That turned out to be real wrong. The following morning, I was in bed watching Snakebite shave. He was a tidy man. All of a sudden, he picked up his pistol, walked outside and shot the poor fella in the back. Walked back in and finished shaving. Weren't no more talk about leaving the gang."

I had another question for Red River John. "What about the Gypsy camp?"

"Mm-hmm. We got a little more than we bargained for there. We rolled in on them but didn't catch them by surprise. There was shooting, but we left in a hurry. Didn't make sense to make a fight with them. Too many, and they had rifles."

"One more question, John. How did you get out alive?"

"Weren't just me. John Doe and Pecos Bill weren't there. Some bounty hunter had them on the way to the law. He didn't get them there. They escaped somehow. Snakebite was fast as lighting. Somehow, during the fight, he jumped the wall. Bordeaux was getting his horse shod when it all happened. Afterward, Snakebite hunted him down and killed him. I'm betting it was a slow death. I guess he thought Bordeaux ran out on them. Hell, I don't really know. Snakebite is crazy. When he feels wronged, he will seek revenge like no-one I ever saw. For me, I had just stepped into the outhouse when all hell broke loose. I broke out the back wall and hid in a draw. Knowing Snakebite like I do, I ran north. Proved to be a mistake."

This is all he had to say that I was interested in. I motioned the guard over. He escorted the man away. This man was a sick and twisted human being. I sat there thinking. Would I rather hang or go to Yuma for life?

Mark Baugher

Getting hanged would be bad, but over quick. Compare that to a dungeon and rotting away for years, I would take the hanging. I was glad he would rot slowly.

Chapter 11
Back on the Hunt

Now that I have you filled in on the Snakebite Gang, I can get back to us hunting them down. There was Uncle Dockie, JL, Eric Alan, Bobby, Big Mike, NoName and myself. We were a formidable bunch. The gang was easy to follow because they had a lot of stolen horses. JL tracked at a distance. The dog kept us informed of possible danger. The trail led us to a miner's cabin. We approached real slow. Out front was a dead man lying in the dirt. Young fella. Just a hard rock miner, trying to make a living. Inside was an older man. Hardly recognizable. He had been shot in the face with a shotgun. Probably got shot when he opened the door. Life had no value to this gang.

That night we were camped when JL spotted a big campfire to the north. We knew it wasn't the gang because they would never make a fire like that.

Uncle Dockie said, "Bobby, Chris, Jessie Lynn and me will see who that is. NoName, you, Big Mike and Eric Alan can follow the gang real slow-like. We will catch up."

The next day, we split up and wandered that way. Before we found whoever was in that camp, we heard someone singing *Amazing Grace*.

Bobby looked saddened and said, "When I hear that song, I know someone died. I got a real bad feeling about this."

When we got there, it was just what we thought. A man and young girl were standing beside a fresh grave. The girl was singing. We held back out of respect. When the song was finished, they realized we were there, and the man turned with a gun in his hand. We were all standing without hats out of respect. He soon saw that we meant them no harm. The man and girl had dirt on their faces and clothes. Their wagon was smoldering. Their belongings were scattered all around.

Uncle Dockie said, "We mean you no harm. We will help you if we can."

The man seemed to be in shock, but he got out, "Summer and I were out gathering firewood. When we got back, they were gone. They killed my wife."

Bobby said, "We know who they are. We are hunting them."

The girl was also in shock but managed to say, "What we gonna do now, Pa?"

The man put his head down with no answer.

Uncle Dockie said gently, "If you need a place to get your life together, you are welcome at out ranch."

JL then said, "Follow the river to the end. That is our ranch. Tell Ma we sent you."

At that point, all we could do was help with the cleanup. We found their horses and got them pointed in the right direction. It was a sad day I will never forget.

Mark Baugher

Chapter 12
Sheriff Comes A-Knockin'

It was mid-afternoon when Sheriff Behan came to the house. Aunt Marsha hated the counterfeit bastard. He pounded on the door.

Aunt Marsha answered. She was not polite. "What do you want?" she barked.

He was just as impolite. "I heard there was trouble out here. Where is Dockie?"

"He's out doing your job."

Then she slammed the door in his face. He left and was not a happy man.

Mark Baugher

Chapter 13
Cim

We were up before the sun the next day and following the trail. Eric Alan, Big Mike and NoName were easy to find so we were riding as one group again.

JL came trotting back. "I smell campfire smoke up ahead."

Uncle NoName said, "May be more pilgrims again."

Uncle Dockie was always who we looked to for direction. "Well, let's do what we did yesterday," he instructed.

So we split up again. We had gotten close enough to smell the smoke, so everyone dismounted and walked. When we got close enough to see what was going on, Uncle Dockie and Bobby smiled at each other. They walked to the camp and we followed. There was one man sleeping, and one woman and two men chained to a tree. Bobby snuck up and took out the cylinder off the sleeping man's gun and put it back in his holster. Then Bobby started up their fire. He dug around the gear laying nearby and found some bacon. He threw the bacon in a frying pan. It was popping and crackling real loud and the smell was damn good also. This made the sleeping man stir. Uncle Dockie and Bobby just stood at his feet, waiting for him to awaken. When he did, it was with a rush and pointing his gun at us.

"Who are you people!!!"

Uncle Dockie said, "Well, hi, Cim. Just old friends."

The man was struggling to see who was standing over him. Then he caught on. "Is that you, Dockie? And Bobby?" He then looked at his gun and saw the cylinder was gone. "You sons of bitches."

Uncle Dockie and Bobby thought that was real funny. Dockie looked past the man and asked, "Who be the woman cuffed to that tree?"

Chained to a juniper tree was a young woman. Could be beautiful in other conditions.

Cim answered, "Just a wanted woman."

Uncle Dockie asked, "What she do?"

"Killed a man."

This surprised Uncle Dockie. "Is that right? Who she kill?"

"Man named Jasper Stone."

This got a laugh out of Uncle Dockie and Bobby.

"I never liked that son of a bitch," said Uncle Dockie. "What kind of bounty's on her head?"

"Fifty dollars," Cim responded.

Uncle Dockie pulled out a roll of bills and handed Cim the fifty dollars. "Can you give me the key to the cuffs?"

Cim reached into his pocket and handed it to Uncle Dockie. He then walked to the young woman. She shrank back in fear. Uncle Dockie stopped short of her and reassured her he meant no harm. He slowly reached to her wrists and unlocked the cuffs and handed her some money. She left at a dead run. We all watched as she ran away.

Uncle Dockie looked concerned about her. "I hope that little ol' girl has somewhere to hide out. Killing Jasper Stone did the world a favor."

Cim said, "What the hell are you boys doing here, anyway?"

Uncle Dockie responded, "Hunting some people. I see you are still hunting bounty."

He shrugged. "Pays the bills. What can I do for you boys?"

Uncle Dockie turned and looked at the two men chained to a tree. "John Doe and Pecos Bill. They run with the people we are hunting."

Cim replied, "I'm sure they would be glad to tell you

what they know if you asked nicely."

Uncle Dockie stared at the men for a few moments, then he demanded, "Where does Snakebite and his gang hang out between raids?"

With contempt, Pecos Bill said, "Ain't got no idea."

Bobby rushed over and grabbed him by the hair, pulling back his head. He pulled a huge knife and put it to the man's throat. "You're going to tell us what we want to know. Just depends how much you suffer before you do." Bobby had a look on his face that was downright terrifying.

Then John Doe started in. He was singing religious songs and quoting the Bible. Man was crazy for sure.

This seemed to embolden Pecos Bill. He spat, "I ain't afraid of you or that big knife."

Bobby put down the knife and walked away. This made Pecos Bill and John Doe break into laughter.

"Ha! I knew he didn't have it in him," said Pecos Bill while John Doe ranted Bible passages.

However, Bobby was not quitting on them. He picked up the frying pan full of frying bacon and walked back. He grabbed Pecos Bill by the hair and held the pan over his head. "How much of this grease do you want me to pour on your face?"

Pecos Bill suddenly lost his attitude. He was yelling, "Don't do it. I'll tell you!!"

John Doe never quit ranting. Uncle Dockie yelled, "Where do they hide out between raids!!"

Scared out of his mind, Pecos Bill responded, "Naco, just over the border."

"Rosa's place?" asked Uncle Dockie.

"Yes. Now let me go."

We had the information we needed, so Bobby turned him loose. Uncle Dockie and Bobby said their goodbyes to Cim and we left. The whole time we did this, John Doe ranted about being there when he got justice served. John Doe was a crazy maniac. I had never seen a more dangerous man.

When we got back to the horses, I asked Bobby about Cim.

"We've known him since we were young. Pretty good ol' boy. Tough as a pine knot. He is a bounty hunter and good at it. Hell, he must be good at it—he had John Doe and Pecos Bill caught. I would like to hear the story on that."

Mark Baugher

Chapter 14
Sheriff Comes A-Knockin' Again

Well into the evening and after dark, Aunt Marsha was inside the ranch house taking care of the girl. She had not spoken so we had no name for her. Aunt Marsha kept her in bed, resting. The girl was a frightened and frazzled woman. Any sound from outside sent her into a panic.

Aunt Marsha brought her some warm soup. "Eat this, hun. You need to build your strength. Tomorrow we will take you to town and buy you some new clothes."

Suddenly there was a banging on the door. From outside came a gruff, "Open the door! I know Dockie's not home. Now, open the damned door!"

Aunt Marsha pulled a pistol out of a drawer and checked to see if it was loaded. While doing this, she yelled back, "Go away! You have no business here."

The door burst open and in came Sheriff Behan. He was drunk and staggering. Behan looked around and saw the girl. "Well, little lady, I need to talk with you."

Aunt Marsha was no weakling. She hit the sheriff on the head with the barrel of the pistol and down he went. When he looked up, all he could see was a mad Marsha Jean.

"Behan, you are lucky Dockie isn't here. He would

kill you. But then again, if he were here, you wouldn't have done this, would you?" Aunt Marsha grabbed the sheriff by the collar and dragged him outside. "Don't come back here, Behan. Be the biggest mistake you ever made."

He crawled to his horse and, with great difficulty, climbed on and rode out. Aunt Marsha never did tell Uncle Dockie. She knew what he would do. Wasn't worth the trouble was her thinking. Just a drunk, after all.

Chapter 15
Gypsy Camp

The farther south we went, the more damage we found. We all stood on a hilltop, looking down at strange wagons and a dozen people. They were burying someone.

Bobby said, "Gypsy camp. Looks like they got hit by Snakebite's gang."

Uncle Dockie just sighed. "Never had good luck with Gypsies. Something always goes wrong in the end."

"We going down to help them?" asked NoName.

"Suppose so," replied Uncle Dockie. "Just don't trust them in any way. If you do, you will regret it."

We rode down slowly. They immediately gathered their weapons and stood ready for trouble.

Bobby called out, "We mean you no harm. Were you attacked?"

An older man stepped forward. "Yes, last evening a group rode in here wanting everything we had. We fought them off. It cost us one dead and one wounded. Do you know about doctoring gunshot wounds?"

Uncle Dockie got off his horse. "I have doctored many wounds. Take me to this person and let me look."

They took Uncle Dockie into a wagon. On the way in, he looked back at us. JL jumped down and followed, more as a guard than help. Wasn't long before he stuck his head out of the wagon.

"Jessie Lynn, get some flat cactus and skin both sides. All we can do with this is help fight off blood poisonin'."

JL moved off into the desert, looking for the cactus. We all dismounted and waited. Wasn't long before she returned and gave the cactus to Uncle Dockie.

He disappeared into the wagon for a few minutes and then returned. "The bullet went through his leg and out the other side. I have put the cactus inside the bandage. It might help."

We were all returning to our horses when an older woman stepped forward. "Young lady, you must not go with them. If you do, you will not return."

JL responded, "Says who?"

"I say so. I have seen a vision. Stay here with us."

It was then that I saw something I have never seen before. Uncle Dockie went into an uncontrolled rage. He started screaming at the old woman. "You filthy, damn, lying Gypsy trash! I'm going to kill you."

He would have if Bobby and NoName had not gotten

between them. Uncle Dockie had pulled his pistol and was aiming it at her. Bobby pushed up the gun and it fired into the air. They managed to wrestle the gun away from Dockie. He was fighting to get at her, and they had their hands full until Big Mike picked him up and carried him out of the camp. After a few minutes, he settled down enough to get on his horse and ride away. He didn't say a word for an hour. JL, Eric Alan and I just looked at each other and shrugged our shoulders.

Uncle Dockie finally turned to us. "I'm sorry for that. Bobby, NoName and Big Mike, thank you for stopping me. I lost my head. Caught me in a soft spot."

He then rode on. At our first opportunity we rode up next to Bobby when he wasn't riding close to Uncle Dockie. I had to ask.

"Bobby, can I ask you a question?"

He didn't respond to the question, he just started explaining. "Strange thing about people. Tell them you know something and they tend to believe you. The Gypsies are real good at it. When that old woman said what she said, I knew Dockie was going to come apart."

JL said, "Uncle Bobby, I still don't understand…"

He didn't speak for a minute or so. I think he was trying to figure out how to explain. Then he said, "When people are told something like that, for some reason they put themselves in a position for it to come true. Your pa knows that. To him it was the same as putting you in a dangerous position. You kids are a soft place for all of us. We don't act with the same composure as we would otherwise."

"But, Uncle Bobby, I didn't believe that old woman."

"But you heard it, and somewhere in your mind, it's there lurking around. Can't be undone now. Our minds are a tricky thing. We have to work on our thinking just like we do everything else in this world."

That was all he had to say about the matter. We didn't talk about it again, but I have spent many hours contemplating the conversation. These old guys are quite the puzzle to me. Not one day of education between them all, and they are still smarter than anyone else I've ever known.

Chapter 16
A Healing Graveside Visit

There is an old family friend we call Uncle Norm. Just like our other "uncles," he's not related. He's just been around a long time and is dear to the family. Uncle Norm had gotten past his years of range work and pretty much stayed close to home and helped with the endless chores that needed to be done. He had a deep voice and was a pleasure to visit with. It was always easier to leave the ranch, knowing he was there to protect the place.

He and Aunt Marsha had been mothering on the girl. She had not said a word yet but seemed to find security in Uncle Norm. She was always more comfortable when he was around, so he stayed close by at all times.

Aunt Marsha had a real scare, so she talked with Uncle Norm about it. "Norm, I found the girl with my pistol in her hands. She found it in a drawer. From the look on her face, I think she was going to use it on herself."

Uncle Norm shook his head as he responded, "Poor girl had a horrible experience. Lost all her family. Probably will never be the same again. A bad experience can ruin a person for life. Let's take her out to the campsite and let her see the graves. Might help if she grieves some."

"Good idea, Norm. I will get her dressed."

"Let me have an hour. I need to go out there first and tidy the place up."

Aunt Marsha got the girl ready and put her on a horse. They rode out to the graves. Uncle Norm said it was the saddest thing he ever saw. The girl walked over to the graves and just stared, probably running everything through her mind. She just stood there, rubbing her wedding ring, with tears running down her cheeks. It did seem to help. After that, she seemed to be a little less distant.

Chapter 17
Mexican Cantina

We were getting closer to Mexico. There were little towns along the way, most very poor. Poverty is an ugly thing. Makes being a human being a difficult experience. As we rode through one of these towns, we found one with a cantina. Uncle Dockie pulled up.

"This cantina would be a place the gang would stop. Let's go in and get some information."

Big Mike said, "If it's all right with everyone, I will stay out here and guard the horses. In a town like this, our horses could disappear real easy."

Then, to his credit, NoName said, "I think it's a good idea if I stay with Big Mike. Places like that always get me started, and we don't need that now."

So, in walked Uncle Dockie, Bobby, Eric Alan, JL and I. We found a typical cantina filled with drunks. JL was the last to enter. The rest of us walked to the bar. As she walked in, a drunk grabbed her butt. He then turned and laughed with his friends. I knew it was going to get rowdy then.

She calmly took off her hat and placed it on the bar. Then she turned and picked up a whiskey bottle. When the offending drunk turned to her, she broke the bottle over his head. Down he went and the fight was on. One of his friends stood up, and she broke a bar stool over his head. I leaned against the bar, watching Eric Alan talk to the bartender while JL tore the place apart. Uncle Dockie, Bobby and Eric Alan didn't even turn to watch.

Eric Alan said to the bartender, "Barkeep, did the Snakebite Gang come in recently?"

The bartender was not comfortable. "Hell, I don't know. People come and go."

Eric Alan grinned. "We are going to sit right here letting my sis tear your place apart. Longer it takes you to tell me what I want to know, the longer your patrons get hell beat out of them. I don't see no whiskey being drunk."

Meanwhile, JL had four of them on the ground and was wailing on a few more. The bartender finally said, "They were here a few hours ago. Left going south is all I know. Now, call off that hellcat."

We began walking out. Uncle Dockie was the last. He called to JL, "Jessie Lynn, quit fooling about. We need to leave."

She knocked one more to the ground. Stood there putting her shirt tail in and getting put back together. Turned and walked out as if this was a daily routine. We saddled up and left town.

Chapter 18
José

The gang was traveling south, and we were less than a day behind them. The Mexican border was close. Uncle Dockie gathered us up.

"We are close to Naco. I will go ahead and look things over. If it's just me, I won't get much attention. I'll be back in an hour."

I didn't like that idea, so I spoke up. "Uncle Dockie, I'm going with you. If there is trouble, you will be damn glad I'm there with Aunt Marsha's shotgun."

NoName commented, "He's right, Dockie."

"Fair enough. Let's ride slow, nephew. We won't arouse suspicion that way."

We rode for thirty minutes without seeing anyone when Uncle Dockie pulled up. In the distance, we could see a rider loping toward us. He had a big round hat, so I was guessing him to be Mexican. As he got closer, I could see Uncle Dockie starting to smile. We sat in the saddle and waited. He was indeed a Mexican vaquero with a big sombrero and proud of his attire. The vaqueros are known for their clothes and gear. Their horsemanship is also the finest you will ever see. I could talk about how he looked for an hour, but I need to get back to the story at hand. The man came to a sliding stop in front of us. He also started to smile.

Uncle Dockie said, "Well, scratch my ass if it ain't an old ghost."

With a Mexican accent, the man replied, "Dockie, the last time I saw you, you and NoName and Bobby and the rest of your compadres were one step ahead of the law and moving cattle north."

Uncle Dockie laughed. "You're right about that, José."

"I have heard that you have a ranch up north and are all settled down."

"Well, I guess you are partly right, but I am here on bad business. I'm hunting Snakebite. He needs killing, and I aim to get the job done."

José chuckled. "You have not settled down then, have you?"

They both laughed.

José then said, "I just came from town. Snakebite and his gang are in the cantina."

"How many men are with him?"

The vaquero got very serious. "Many. I don't think it's a good idea for you and one more to go up against them."

C-Bar

Uncle Dockie smiled. "The other boys ain't far."

They looked at each other and reached out to shake hands. "Amigo," said José.

"My old friend and amigo," said Dockie.

We rode on towards town. The closer we got, the more I could tell this was a border town. Poverty was everywhere. People lived in squalor. We saw no evidence of the law. This was a perfect place for gangs to hide out. Uncle Dockie pulled up to a blacksmith and tied off to a hitching post. Uncle Dockie rattled off Mexican to him and handed the blacksmith a coin. We then walked down the street. Uncle Dockie commented,
 "Just ahead is an outdoor cantina. High walls surround it. I suspect it's where they are. Let's walk in and have a drink."

This was getting scary. We boldly walked into the cantina and to the bar. A beautiful Mexican woman was singing on the stage. There were twenty or thirty people there. At the north end was a group of people sitting around some tables. They were drunk and loud. Didn't seem to notice us. We ordered a drink.

The bartender looked us over. Quietly, the man said, "Barnett, you must be crazy to be in here."

Uncle Dockie stared back at the man. "Do I know you?"

"No, but I know who you are. I spent time in Prescott. I hope you didn't come here to cause trouble."

"Don't want trouble. Just passing through on a cattle buying trip. You'll never see me again."

The bartender looked relieved and nodded his head. We tossed back our drinks, then left. We had the layout now.

When we got back to everyone waiting, Uncle Dockie spoke to the group.

"They are in the cantina. At least a dozen of them. Luckily for us, they are drunk. Here's the plan—I walk in first; you all follow. We line up and let loose with shotguns as fast as we can. Don't quit firing until they are all dead. Any friend of this group is trash and deserves to die. We all wear a scarf over our faces. We don't want any survivors knowing who we are."

NoName grabbed Jessie Lynn and Eric Alan. "Kids, you need to stay in line. If you walk out in front, you will be between us and them. Bad place to be. You would draw their fire, and we could shoot you in the back by mistake."

They nodded their understanding, and off we rode. Seven road-dirty people riding into town with masks over their faces got a lot of quick looks. They the townspeople darted into whatever building they could find.

We tied up and walked right in the front door of the cantina. The Mexican woman was still singing. JL was mad as hell and didn't follow orders. She wanted to start the killing. We all walked in and lined up in front of the north end tables. JL walked forward and started shooting. All hell broke loose. The seven of us were firing point blank into the crowd with ten-gauge shotguns. Was it murder? Hell, yes, it was. We didn't care. People were running in every direction. The gunsmoke was getting too thick to see clearly. Snakebite was hiding behind an overturned table. One of the gang stood up to fight back. He got all our attention for a moment. He died in a hail of buckshot.

This was the opportunity Snakebite was waiting for. He darted out and was over the wall with buckshot hitting all around him. There was still some resistance, and they were shooting from behind tables. JL walked out to get a better shot at them, which made us stop shooting because we were afraid of hitting her.

That's when Snakebite popped up from behind the wall and shot JL in the chest and then he was gone. The blood flew in the air. Uncle Dockie caught her before she hit the ground. NoName and Uncle Dockie had her in their arms while the rest of us finished them off. We killed fourteen bandits in all. Dead bodies were everywhere. We had one who was shot, and she was shot bad. We were all beside ourselves. Dockie was yelling Mex talk in the air. He was yelling for a doctor.

Mark Baugher

C-Bar

Chapter 19
Uncle Norm's New Friend

The girl found comfort in Uncle Norm. He was gentle and quiet with her. They spent many hours sitting on the porch in silence. She still wasn't talking, but Uncle Norm was all right with that. He didn't push her in any way. It got so that when Uncle Norm would leave to do anything, she tagged along like a shadow. Whichever chores he did, she was right beside him, not helping, but just close.

Uncle Norm waited patiently. They sat in silence, while Uncle Norm rolled a cigarette. He noticed her watching intently. He offered it to her and she took it. Uncle Norm could tell she was a smoker, so he struck a match. The girl put the cigarette in her mouth and leaned toward the match. The cigarette lit and the girl inhaled deeply. She looked at Uncle Norm with a look of thank you. He leaned closer to her and asked quietly, "What is your name?"

A few seconds later, she responded, "Sara."

He gave her a warm smile. "Well, it's a pleasure to meet you, Sara."

They both drifted back into silence, enjoying their smokes.

C-Bar

Chapter 20
The Doctor

JL had lost a lot of blood. She was drifting in and out of consciousness. Uncle Dockie and NoName were covered in her blood. We heard about a doctor living on the edge of town. NoName and Uncle Dockie carried her until we came across a man driving a buckboard wagon. With six well-armed and desperate people yelling at him, he stopped and told us he would take everyone to the doctor. He pulled in front of the doctor's house and stopped.

Uncle Dockie ran inside, yelling, "The doctor! Where is the Goddamn doctor?!"

Noname was right behind him, carrying JL, and we were all right there also.

A woman walked out of a back room. "Settle down. The doctor is with another patient."

"I don't give a damn! Get his ass out here right now!"

It was then that NoName entered, carrying JL. Both were covered in blood. The nurse took very little time to see the urgency.

"Oh, Lord, bring her in here. Bring her now."

We crowded into the exam room. NoName put JL on the table.

JL was talking out of her head. "Pa, Pa, help me, Pa…" We were all scared to death.

The doctor barged in. "Get out of the way! Make room." He started looking over JL's wounds. He was trying to stop the bleeding. We were all yelling at the doctor to help her.

He turned to Uncle Dockie. "She has lost too much blood."

This hit us all like a rock. Uncle Dockie looked at the doctor. "Is she going to live?"

The doctor shook his head no.

I thought Uncle Dockie was going to pass out. NoName pulled his pistol, pointed it at the doctor and growled, "Doc, if she dies—"

Bobby pulled him off the doctor. "Let's go outside. We ain't doing no good here."

Bobbie led NoName out to the porch and sat him in a chair. NoName cried like a baby. Bobby just sat and stared at his bloody hands. Eric Alan was pacing the porch with hatred in his eyes. He was watching for any of the gang who might be coming for us.

The doctor looked gravely at Uncle Dockie and said, "She has only one chance. We can pump some blood from you into her. Are you her real pa?"

Uncle Dockie just nodded his head. He was in shock.

The doctor instructed his nurse, "Blood transfusion." She ran off to get the equipment. The doctor turned back to Uncle Dockie and said, "You being her pa is a good thing. Your blood may match up. If not, what we are going to do may kill her, but it's her only chance to live through this. Do you want me to do this?"

Again, Uncle Dockie just nodded his head. The nurse came in with hoses and a shiny pump. The doctor took one end of a hose and attached a needle to it. He then put it in JL's arm. With the other end, he did the same in Uncle Dockie's arm. The doctor started working the pump. He did that for a while but then he stopped.

Uncle Dockie asked, "Why you stopping?"

He replied, "Because if I take too much it can kill you."

Uncle Dockie pulled his pistol and pointed it at the doctor. "Don't worry about me. Take what Jessie Lynn needs to survive!"

The doctor just shrugged and kept pumping.

C-Bar

Chapter 21
Three Months Later

Uncle Dockie looked like hell. He hadn't shaved since the gunfight. He never went to the ranch house. He just prowled the countryside. JL had survived that fateful day and healed up fairly well. She was worried sick about him. She came to me one day.

"Chris, I'm right worried about Pa. He just keeps patrolling the countryside. Lost weight, doesn't clean up. He's gettin' old and can't keep this up."

"JL, all I can tell you is the world ain't been able to kill him yet. I think he knows what he's doing."

"Well, I'm going to go get him and make him come home."

"Hmph. Good luck with that, cuz. He won't come in and he won't let you stay. He's almost as stubborn as someone else I know."

She stormed away toward her horse.

She found Uncle Dockie sitting on a hillside, watching a canyon through a long looking glass. When JL walked up to him, he didn't take his eyes away from the long glass. He just lifted his arm so she could sit beside him while he put his arm around her. He then looked at her.

"Nice to see you, sweetheart."

"Nice to see you, Pa."

"You do know, Jessie Lynn, that you can't stay."

"Yes, I know. You ain't looking so good."

He responded, "I'm fine, I'm fine."

"Well, you are the poorest 'fine' I ever saw."

He just smiled.

"When you coming home, Pa?"

He responded, "When this is all over."

JL was getting choked up. "Snakebite has moved on. He ain't coming back."

Uncle Dockie thought for a moment and then said, "I know this kind of man. He is coming back, and it will be soon."

JL just looked confused. "How the hell you know that?"

"I was raised in a little ol' Mexican village. Didn't know that, did you?"

"No, Pa. There is a lot I don't know."

"We had to deal with people like him—bandits from both sides of the border and Apaches. They made life real hard."

JL put her head down. "I'm sorry you had to go through that, Pa."

He looked at JL and pulled her close. "I don't want you to feel that way. I'm the luckiest man in the world. I got you, don't I?"

JL smiled. They just sat for a minute or two. Uncle Dockie then said, "Jessie Lynn, how is your arm?"

"It's fine."

A short time passed without any words. Uncle Dockie was about to nod off when he said, "I need to put my head back and take a little nap. Maybe you can keep an eye out for me."

He tried to lay his head on a rock. JL took off her coat and lifted his head enough to put the coat under his head. She made her pa comfortable, picked up the long glass and kept watch.

C-Bar

Chapter 22
NoName

NoName was known for his drinking binges. He would get roaring drunk and go visit the ranch and entertain anyone available. Lovable and loyal to a fault, he was. People worried about him falling off his horse and hitting his head or freezing to death and no-one would know until we saw the buzzards circling. Aunt Marsha nagged him about it but to no avail.

A few days after JL had visited her pa and had gone back to the ranch, I went out to go with Uncle Dockie on his rounds. Uncle Dockie accepted me and continued his watch. We were coming around a little hill when Uncle Dockie's horse spooked and almost threw him off. My horse didn't respond as violently. When we got our horses under control, we looked for what had caused the problem.

Under a tree sat NoName. His hands were tied over his head. NoName's stomach had been cut open and his intestines were hanging out. I was in disbelief and shock. Uncle Dockie looked ready to collapse. We dismounted and walked over to NoName. Uncle Dockie sat down beside him. He drew a knife and cut the rope holding his hands in the air. He pulled NoName to his chest and rested his chin on NoName's forehead. NoName's eyes fluttered open and he groaned. My God, he was still alive! Uncle Dockie put his ear down to hear what NoName was trying to say. When he pulled away, he had tears running down his cheeks. He kissed

C-Bar

NoName on the forehead, pulled his pistol and shot NoName through the heart.

To this day, I still cry when thinking about what Uncle Dockie did for his old friend, NoName. Uncle Dockie gently laid him down and just looked at him. He then started to gag and began throwing up. When his stomach was empty, he rolled over and laid his head in NoName's lap and wept.

Chapter 23
Bunny

JL, Eric Alan and Uncle Bobby were doing some riding, looking for any sign of Snakebite. They saw nothing much to be concerned about. Toward dark and three miles from the house, Uncle Bobby's horse did a big spook and a complete spin around. They started looking for the cause when JL gasped. In our part of the country it's not uncommon to see an ant hill several feet high. However, next to it was a man staked out on the ground. I had heard that the Apaches would do this but never saw it. The man was dead but recognizable. Uncle Bobby had to study him for a while but then his eyes got real big.

JL was wanting answers. "Who is that, Uncle Bobby?"

He answered, "They called him Bunny. He rode with the Snakebite Gang. He wasn't at the shootout that day. I always regretted not killing him with the rest of that trash. I heard that Snakebite does this kind of thing to anyone he feels is disloyal to their gang. Let's get home and alert everyone. Snakebite is close..."

Everyone loped their horses toward the ranch house.

C-Bar

Chapter 24
Sara

Sara was doing better every day. She seemed to be coming back to the world of the living. She let Uncle Norm get farther away. Aunt Marsha was mothering her night and day. After dark, Sara slept in the bed we put in the main room. She was not ready to be off by herself in another room just yet.

It was just the two of them in the house, as Norm was out doing chores. The stove needed firewood, so Aunt Marsha went out the back door to get an armload. She had not been gone long when the front door was opened very quietly. Snakebite slipped in and stood quietly, taking in the room. Sara was asleep in bed. He slowly climbed on the bed and straddled her. He pulled a long, pointed object from his belt. Sara opened her eyes and started to scream, but Snakebite grabbed a pillow and covered her face. Her screams were muffled. He then ran the long, pointed knife through the pillow and into her eye. He pushed down while Sara struggled for a few seconds and finally went lifeless.

Snakebite was grinning and enjoyed this horrible act. He heard someone coming, so he jumped off and hid behind a large dresser. Aunt Marsha entered and threw the firewood in the wood box. She turned to see a bloody pillow and object sticking out of it covering Sara's face. She screamed and then Snakebite lunged at her. They scuffled until Snakebite grabbed her hair and threw her to the floor. He stood over her with a knife, ready to stab

Aunt Marsha, when he was hit from behind. Uncle Norm had heard the noise and came running. He had grabbed a chunk of firewood and hit Snakebite in the back of the head.

JL, Eric Alan and Bobby came running in to find Snakebite on the floor with Uncle Norm beating him with the firewood. The three of them also got in some kicks of their own.

Chapter 25
Saying Goodbye

Snakebite was chained hand and foot and thrown in a root cellar. An hour later, Uncle Dockie and I came rolling in at a run. We sat up all night talking. Uncle Norm and I went out the next day to pick up NoName and bring him back. We took him and Sara out to our little graveyard. Two graves were dug and both gently placed in the ground with blankets covering them. We filled in the graves and we all stood there in our grief.

Bobby spoke and was noticeably saddened. "NoName was born in a whore house in Tucson. All he knew was dirt, cold and fear. There were several of us no better off. NoName was loyal, cheerful and always full of life. He said the only reason he cared to survive was because of Marsha Jean and the kids. A man could not have a better friend. Rest in peace, my friend."

Uncle Norm added, "Happy trails, my friend."

All we could do then was go home and get busy. The next morning, Uncle Dockie came to get me. "Chris, would you help me this morning?"

I jumped up and followed Uncle Dockie to the cellar we had Snakebite caged in. Uncle Dockie pulled him out. He then put a bag over his head and a rope around his neck. We saddled up and rode out with Snakebite running behind us. He couldn't see, so he was stumbling and falling. Uncle Dockie didn't give him any help getting up. He just led the stumbling and falling man out into the trees. When we got to where we were going, there were two shovels waiting for us.

"Chris, would you help me dig a shallow grave?"

We dug for about an hour and got down about three feet.

"Good enough, Chris. If you don't want to see this, I understand."

"I'm here to help, Uncle Dockie."

Uncle Dockie then went over and dragged Snakebite to the grave. He threw him in with Snakebite landing on his knees. He pulled the hood off his head.

Uncle Dockie gazed up to the clouds. "When I was a young man, I would have just shot you and pushed you into that hole. I would have looked up to the Lord and said, 'One less.' But I'm older now, and the questions have piled up."

Uncle Dockie sat beside Snakebite with his feet in the grave. His face was very close to Snakebite when he said, "Were you born this way or treated poorly? Are you evil or a victim of your circumstances? If I took you home and treated you with kindness, would you see me as weak? Should I hate you or feel sorry for you? Will the Lord hold me accountable for what I'm about to do? You see, I wonder about things like this."

He paused for a bit and sighed, then said, "I'll tell you what I believe. The Lord knows I can't let you live. When my days are over and I'm standing in front of the Lord and we discuss how I handled my life, I think I'm going to get this question: *Dockie, did you enjoy killing the man?* It won't speak well for me when I answer 'yes.'"

Uncle Dockie then got up and out of the grave. He threw the shovel aside and walked behind Snakebite. He pulled his pistol and blew Snakebite's brains out. Snakebite slumped into the grave.

I said quietly, "Uncle Dockie, why don't you go on back to the house? Your family needs you. I can finish here."

He nodded his head, walked to his horse, mounted and rode away. I just stared at this now-dead man. He caused so much pain and suffering in the world. Uncle Dockie's questions rambled through my mind.

I filled in the grave and went home—home to family and friends, the only thing that makes this life any different than that of a wild animal. I know we all take the good with the bad. I went home to love on all my family. We all needed that very badly.

C-Bar

Chapter 26
Living with the Past

Uncle Dockie was deeply disturbed with having to put NoName out of his misery. He grew steadily more quiet and reserved. Spent a lot of time alone. We were all very worried. Around dinner one evening, we had a discussion.

JL spoke first. "Pa is a mess. Won't talk about what is troubling him. Gone most of the time. I'm worried. What you think is bothering him, Ma?"

"He won't talk to me, either, but I know him having to kill NoName is eating his heart out. They grew up together and fought to survive. Their bond is as strong as family. Poor man was put in a bad place. Let NoName suffer, or help him out of life and then live with what he did. I can't even imagine his guilt."

Aunt Marsha broke down crying and so did a few more at the table. Uncle Norm added, "What your pa is suffering from is what we called melancholy. Saw it after the war. Some people suffer more than others. Ain't no cure. He will either come through it or waste away. All we can do is be there for him."

Let me tell you this—I don't like not being able to help a loved one. I wanted to get mad. I wanted to tell him he did all he could do. It wasn't his fault. My mind went on and on with how to make him understand and forgive himself. I remember Uncle Dockie telling me

C-Bar

once, "Ain't no use arguing with someone. You will never change their mind." I had never felt so helpless in my life.

I was not there for the rest of this story. Uncle Dockie sat with me one afternoon and related what happened. Our relationship is that of family now, so I have his confidence. I will tell you the tale as if I were there.

***

Uncle Dockie was sitting on the bank of the Wet Beaver Creek that runs to the east of the C-Bar. It's a bigger river then the Verde River that runs through the C-Bar Ranch. It's a beautiful place. Red sandstone rocks and boulders. High cliffs with huge cottonwood trees. The canyon is sometimes steep and narrow.

The Apache people had been there for a thousand years or more. The beauty was breathtaking. White men avoided this area because the Apache people were still there and held the area as sacred. A narrow trail ran the side of a mountain that led to the river. It was steep and narrow, the kind of trail that if your horse spooks and goes over the edge, you know for sure you will not survive. I personally loved the place, but danger was everywhere and to lose your focus would get you killed.

Uncle Dockie was depressed to his core. He was wandering with no purpose, and I suspected he was looking to get out of this world via a last battle with his lifelong foe, the Apache. He had fought them since childhood and respected them as well as hating them.

I have told you the story about me losing Barney Martin and his family. They were all brutally murdered. In my grief, I walked into a saloon and murdered the man who killed him and his family. I was out of my head when Uncle Dockie found me. JL didn't understand what was going on with me. Uncle Dockie told her, "Sometimes the world gives you more than you can carry." That is just what happened to Uncle Dockie. He had more than he could carry and was looking for relief. He knew you can't run away from memories. When things are done, they are done, and then the hard part is living with the memory. This just comes with living a long life.

He was sitting there, absorbed in his grief and guilt. Thoughts of the gunfight and JL getting shot. Remembering how he found NoName and doing what he did for him. Executing Snakebite. The memories would just not go away. They were only getting worse. He was haunted day and night. There was a noise that brought him back to the world. The sound was his horse snorting. A horse will tell you if something or someone is approaching. He slowly turned and could see an Apache warrior on horseback. The warrior was moving slowly and carefully. This told Uncle Dockie that they knew he was there. In a flash, he was on his horse and running.

Dockie was flying through the river's underbrush. He knew the race was on. To be caught alive was a nightmare, so fighting to the death was the only option. Dockie was probably there for just that. He burst out of the brush into the open. Six warriors were close behind. Even in his dead-out run, he admired them. A beautiful and magnificent people. No better warriors existed, and all were exceptional horsemen.

But ol' Dockie had some tricks, some of which, ironically, he learned from the Apache. He could lean off the left side of the horse with his elbow around the saddle horn. This let him look back and fire his pistol with his right hand. This kept the warriors backed off. Hitting a target in this fashion is almost impossible, but the warriors knew about luck and they were not willing to chance a lucky shot. They held back.

Dockie's horse was giving its all. A horse will do that, unlike a mule. A horse will run itself to death. Dockie was weighing all the odds. He knew the horse could not do this forever, so he was looking for a place to fort up. His horse was starting to lose this race, so he just rode into the brush and dismounted. He gathered his rifle and ran for a log next to the river. He would die here if necessary.

The Apache were too wily to come crashing in after him. They held back to talk. It became obvious that there we two young warriors wanting to rush in. The older men were trying to talk them out of it, but on the two came. They hit the brush at the same time. Dockie killed them both with ease.

They lay in the brush as Dockie wondered how young people survive at all. There were no options for Dockie now. The four remaining warriors would dismount and scatter around him. The only option was to run—and run for his life. He crawled up to one of the dead warriors and removed his leather moccasins. They had high tops that laced to the knee. Perfect for running, unlike the boots he was wearing. Dockie removed his chaps and boots, replacing them with the moccasins. The rifle was heavy, but he decided to carry it for a short time.

The canyon walls were steep, too steep for horses, so Dockie started climbing. The warriors had to go slowly, so it took them some time to figure out Dockie's path. Dockie found the trail leading to the river about halfway up the cliffside. He got there, rested and waited.

C-Bar

Chapter 27
The Big Dance

There was a big dance in town that Saturday evening. Uncle Norm decided that everyone needed to go and have some fun. Everyone at the ranch was in a worry about Dockie, so it was time to distract their minds. He called a meeting.

"This place needs some fun. We are all going to town to the dance tonight. No excuses."

JL looked at her ma. "Ma, you going to the dance with us?"

"I don't think so. I will stay here and take care of the children. Besides, your pa may come home, and I want to be here if he does.

Good ol' Winston then said, "I'm not really in the mood for a party. I will stay home with Ma."

We all knew he was staying with ma rather than leave her on the ranch alone. The rest of us agreed that we needed some time away, so off we went. Prescott was a lively place that night. There was Uncle Norm, Uncle Bobby, JL, Eric Alan and myself. We blended right in. The dance was in a huge brick building. It could hold at least a hundred people. The sheriff was checking all guns at the door. On the stage was a band and a singer. Who were they? You guessed it—Clay Boy, Little Ned and their band. The town loved them. Little Ned was good at calling out dances. Square dances, the Virginia Reel and the like had everyone involved.

It was time to let loose, and we did. JL was always popular to dance with so she never got to sit down. To the side of the floor was a bar lined up with spiked punch. Of course, there were the usual drunks.

One young buck walked up to JL and said something in her ear. I knew this was going to be interesting, so I grabbed Eric Alan by his sleeve and whispered, "Your big sister is about to do what she does so well."

We knew her and recognized a response that usually led to someone getting hurt. However, on this occasion, she immediately changed expression and smiled. She nodded toward the door and walked out. The young buck was strutting as he followed her out. He was expecting a warm moment.

Just before leaving, she bumped into a deputy. The deputy didn't realize it, but he no longer had his pistol. The young buck was just walking out and rounding the corner when his head flew back and down he went. JL walked back in and handed the deputy his pistol. The deputy then realized he was being handed his own gun. He had a big look of surprise. JL walked in and grabbed Uncle Norm like it never happened. Eric Alan and I were greatly amused.

***

Dockie, meanwhile, had the advantage for the moment. The Apache warriors were still figuring things out. The mistake they made was showing themselves. Dockie took careful aim and fired. Blood flew out of the back of one of the warriors. He fell to the ground. They were going to discover Dockie's location eventually, so he just took advantage of the moment. The rest of them scattered and hid behind boulders. It was only a matter of time before they crawled to either side, so Dockie emptied his rifle on them. Lead bullets splatter when they hit rocks, so Dockie played with this for a while.

Finally, he stood and yelled, "I have killed your people all my life. Your fathers and grandfathers have been trying to kill me. I have always been the better warrior. Leave, or I will kill you also!"

Dockie knew that running was the only way out and carrying a ten pound rifle uphill was a bad idea. He threw it behind a boulder and ran. His youth was behind him. Age robs people of their strength, but there was still life in ol' Dockie. The warriors soon figured out he had run, so they were in hot pursuit.

***

The band had played its last song, so the crowd was slowly leaving. It was a wonderful and needed evening. We sat and visited with Brandy and Clay about Uncle Dockie. It was getting late, so we walked toward the wagon. We were met by the idiot JL had given an etiquette lesson to. He walked up and punched JL in the face. This could possibly be the dumbest thing I had ever seen. Bobby was enraged. He tore into the man with everything he had. He quickly had him on the ground and was pounding his face.

JL was up quick and yelling, "Help me get Uncle Bobby off the man or he will kill him!"

It took all of us to pull Bobby off. He was wide-eyed and crazy-looking.

JL got right in his face. "I am all right, Uncle Bobby. I'm not hurt!"

She repeated this several times before Bobby calmed down. He took her face in his hands and asked, "Sweetheart, are you hurt?"

"No, I'm fine, Uncle Bobby."

We walked away, leaving a bloody and beaten young man lying in the dirt.

***

Dockie was in good shape but no match for young warriors in their prime. They were gaining steadily. Dockie was running on a straight part of the trail when he was hit in the side by a rifle bullet. Down he went, rolling in the dirt, but was up immediately and running. He didn't know how badly he was injured, but he didn't have the time to inspect the wound. He was, however, tiring and losing strength.

The trail had a sheer cliff on one side and a drop off on the other. There was only one way to move forward. The trail had a sharp turn. Dockie made the turn and sat on the path to rest. The wound was not as bad as it could have been but only because of his gun belt. The heavy leather helped deflect the bullet. The blood was running down his hip and leg. Dockie sat and waited. He rolled a cigarette and inhaled the smoke. He loved a good smoke from time to time.

The warriors approached the bend in the trail slowly, knowing they were at a disadvantage. When they got close, a puff of smoke let them know Dockie was there and waiting. The small war party was led by a man called Loco Moon. He stood quietly and listened. From behind the boulder, he heard Spanish, a language he understood.

"If you come any closer, you will die."

Loco Moon smiled. "You are bleeding. We can wait."

"What is your name?"

"They call me Loco Moon. Are you the one they call Blanco Nino?"

"That be me."

"My father was also called Loco Moon. You killed

him."

"Yes, I did. Your father was a brave warrior. I sure would like to kill me a few more Apaches like him before I die. Trouble is all you young warriors ain't even close to what your fathers were."

"Old man, I may be the one who kills you."

Dockie paused. "Here I am, a dying man, and the last thing I want to do is kill more of your people. Seems like a poor way to go out of this world."

Loco Moon thought for a moment. "Killing white people is what I live for. I do not wish to die an old man like you. I wish to die a warrior."

Dockie replied, "I understand. When I was young like you, I felt the same way. Now I am old and sometimes think differently."

"I will die killing the white men. Your people have killed most of my people. I hate you to my soul."

"Your people have killed many of my loved ones also. My heart, too, is filled with hate. When I was young, I carried the hatred with ease. Now it is a burden. It is as if we have jumped off a tall cliff. Once done it cannot be undone. I ask God to take the hatred from my heart, but He does not listen to me."

Loco Moon spoke with contempt. "You are old and

weak! No longer the warrior the old people talk about in my village."

Dockie took a deep breath. "Maybe so. Sometimes I see how things could be but probably will never be. I am tired and will speak no more. I will wait for you."

Loco Moon and his warriors waited patiently. They could see the smoke from Dockie's cigarette drifting by. A few minutes passed. One of the younger warriors became impatient and looked around the corner. Dockie was gone. Only a cigarette was sitting on a rock, slowly burning. They knew he was up and running again.

C-Bar

Chapter 28
Seeing Ghosts

When we got back to the wagon we were all subdued. The fight had taken the joy from the evening. It was one of those moonlit nights that is so bright you can read a book by it. Beautiful night. We were leaving town when a figure stepped out of a shadow. There were several pistols pointing at the figure in a flash.

"Please do not shoot me. It is only me, José. Bobby, surely you remember me?"

I recognized him from when Uncle Dockie and I were scouting the town before the gunfight. We ran into this man, his old friend. Bobby was off the wagon and shaking hands with José. They slapped each other on the back for a moment.

"José, my old friend! Why are you here in the dark?"

"Bobby, I have come to warn you of danger. After the gunfight, John Doe is swearing revenge. He is gathering people to come kill your family."

"When are they coming?"

"He said with the next full moon."

I jumped in and asked, "How many?"

José looked worried. "He has nine now. How many

more by that time, I cannot tell you. I must go now before anyone sees me talking with you. I would surely die if John Doe were to find out. He has spies everywhere."

The old man faded into the shadows.

***

Dockie was still running, but not as fast. He had a head start, but he was losing ground. The trail ended at a cliff overlooking the river. Thirty feet below was a large pool of water. How deep was impossible to tell. Dockie stopped and peeked over the edge. A rifle shot rang out and Dockie was thrown over the side. He fell the great distance and went under the water. The warriors ran to the cliff edge and looked down. Dockie's body was drifting with the river current and disappeared around the bend.

Loco Moon smiled with satisfaction. "I have killed Blanco Nino. My forefathers are smiling. Let's get his body to take back to the village."

Dockie floated down river for a hundred yards. He was hitting a shallow area when a woman jumped into the water and pulled him to the bank and then into the deep brush. There she examined his wounds. They were not severe enough to kill him, if she could stop the bleeding, which she worked on. Dockie opened his eyes and saw her.

"You are the young woman that Cim was taking in to the law."

She just nodded her head. She could hear the warriors on the other side of the river. She covered his mouth and waited with a pistol pointing toward the sounds of the warriors. They passed, and she waited with Dockie's head in her lap. The warriors never came back.

***

On the way home, we were all quiet. I am sure everyone was planning our defenses. I had my own plan. When we got back to the ranch, everyone else went to bed, but I waited for a while. I then gathered up the shotgun and my trail clothes. I was going to kill John Doe before he could get here. One man could get done what several couldn't. My plan was to walk into the cantina, figure out which one he was, and blow him to Hell. They might get me, but that was better than more of my loved ones.

I left a note and headed south. I knew the way because I had been there before. Three days later, I was looking at Naco, Mexico. I tied my horse to a tree among other horses. I didn't want to draw attention. There was a general store, so I went in to find something to cover myself with. A big sombrero and cape would help me blend in. Aunt Marsha's shotgun was well hidden under the cape. It was close to dark, and I was hoping not to be noticed. The open-air cantina looked just the same. I walked in and went to the end of the bar. There was a side door within a few feet.

The bartender came for my order. "What will you have, señor?"

"Beer," I replied curtly.

He was looking me over real hard. He left and returned with the drink, then he said quietly, "Señor, I know who you are. You are crazy to be here. Please leave. I don't want my place shot up again."

"I will leave when you point out John Doe to me."

"He is not here, señor! Please leave. They are looking at you right now."

The bartender walked away and suddenly ducked behind the bar. I knew I was spotted. I swung toward the table of men and let loose with both barrels. Some went down and the rest scattered. I dove for the door and out I went, running as fast as I could.

The alarm went up. I had failed. People were looking everywhere for me. All I did was stir up a hornets' nest. I was in deep trouble and hiding in an alley.

A Mexican woman walked my way. She motioned to me. "Señor, you must follow me," she whispered.

All my choices were gone, so I decided to trust her. She led me to a small house and I followed her in. She lit a lamp and I knew who she was—the Mexican woman who was singing in the cantina.

In my panic, I asked as we walked along the alley, "Why are you helping me?"

"When you were here last, you killed the man who owned me. You set me free."

I now understood. "What is your name?"

"Annabelle."

"What will happen to you now?"

"Another man will own me."

I shook my head. "That ain't going to happen. You're going with me. We will wait an hour and then leave town."

"I cannot go with you. I have a daughter I must care for. She is asleep in the bedroom. Where is your horse?"

I said, "My horse is tied to a tree on Main Street."

"You cannot go back there," she said. "I will take you to the stable for a horse and show you a way out of town."

We slipped out the door. She took me to the stable. When I entered the owner stopped me. "What do you want!" he growled.

I looked him in the eye and said, "Good horse and saddle. If I don't get it, you die!"

He knew I was desperate and got to work. I was surprised at the horse he brought me. It was beautiful.

"Señor, what is wrong with this horse? If it is not rideable, I will come back and kill you!"

He smiled. "This is a fine horse. It belongs to John Doe. I cannot help it if you snuck in and stole it." He winked at me.

I knew the stable owner would not sound the alarm, so I passed him a double eagle. Annabelle and I stayed in the shadows and finally reached the edge of town. I turned to thank her when her chest exploded. Poor woman was dead before she hit the ground. I mounted and left town on a dead run.

***

The woman managed to get Dockie to a safe place. He was out of his head with delirium. Later on, Uncle Dockie told me he had been walking down a trail and not well when he ran right into NoName.

"NoName is that you?"

"Sure is, Dockie. You look like hell."

"I've been better. How are you?"

"Doing just fine, Dockie. Better than ever. I hope you know you're walking in the wrong direction if you are going home."

Then Dockie was suddenly feeling fine. *"NoName, remember when we were young bucks thinking we could conquer the world? We had great fun, didn't we?"*

"Yes, we did, Dockie. The world let us know otherwise, didn't it?"

They were laughing and walking arm in arm down the trail. Life was free and easy again.

***

I was making good time and stopped to let the horse rest. I was hoping I was not being followed, but I was wrong. Gun shots rang out and the dirt all around me was throwing up clouds of dust. I climbed on my horse, gathered up the reins and kicked him into a dead run. How close they were I couldn't tell, but I knew they were close. John Doe's horse was fading fast so I turned into a canyon. Was it smart or not, I didn't know, but I had to fort up. I rode around a corner and dismounted. The horse was tired and wouldn't go far, so I let him loose. I grabbed my shotgun and lay behind a boulder, waiting. It wasn't long before they caught up. They knew better then to blindly take the sharp turn, so they stopped to think. I only had my shotgun, but they didn't know that. I decided to take a chance.

"John Doe, you out there?"

"Yes, I am, you son of a bitch! You stole my horse. I plan on killing you today."

"Well, John, come on in and do just that. My Winchester plays some mighty good music for people like you."

"We are in no hurry. We'll just wait a spell. God is on my side, and I will see justice."

I peeked around the bolder and saw him talk with two of the gang. They peeled off to the north at a dead run. I knew he was sending them around to block me from going somewhere so I took a chance, mounted and flew down the canyon. Much to my relief, I came to a wide opening that led to the open country. Out I went. I never saw any of them following me, so I figured they had decided it was not worth their time to follow.

I headed home a much beaten man. Three days later, I arrived. When I got back, I saw Dockie sitting on the porch, not looking well. JL came out to fill me in.

"Pa just showed up, lying on the porch one morning. Shot twice and bandaged up by someone. "

"Who brought him home?"

"We have no idea."

"What does he have to say?"

"He ain't talking," she said. "Ma says not to push."

Now this was a puzzle. For the next week, Uncle Dockie just sat there. Then one day, Uncle Norm was sitting on one side and Aunt Marsha on the other. JL was sitting on the ground between Dockie's knees. He was getting a lot of love and support from someone every minute of the day. No one was talking much. Aunt Marsha must have thought it was the right time to broach the subject.

She asked, "Dockie, what happened out there?"

He looked at her for a long time and finally broke his silence. "I found trouble down on Wet Beaver Creek. NoName found me and got me going in the right direction. He sure looked good. Better than I have seen him in years."

Uncle Norm looked at Uncle Dockie with worry. "You do know that NoName is dead…?"

I thought at the time that Norm should not have said that. It was just too much for Uncle Dockie to hear. But, looking back, I think it's just what Uncle Dockie needed at that time. Still, the hard truth can sometimes be a hard pill to swallow.

The entire idea of NoName being dead appeared to be a big shock to Uncle Dockie. He stared for a minute and then his head dropped. Tears flowed down his cheeks. His head was bobbing. Aunt Marsha pulled him to her while he cried. JL sat there with her chin on his leg and couldn't help but cry also. It was tough to watch. Thank God this family is there for each other. I don't know how a person gets through life without help.

The next day, JL came looking for us all. Uncle Dockie needed to talk with us. We gathered up at the house and Uncle Dockie came out. He looked better. Hurt, but getting around.

He said, "It's time to get ready for John Doe. We have some people to kill. Let's go to the house and make a plan." We all crowded into the house where Dockie continued, "You all know that we have been warned about John Doe seeking revenge. An old friend said he is gathering more people like him for a raid on us at the next full moon. We need to start getting ready."

It was decided that a constant guard needed to be on duty. People needed to ride about a half-mile out and circle the ranch going in opposite directions. If they didn't cross paths, it would be a sign that one of them was in trouble. We also needed people on guard at all times in the ranch area. We were told that he was coming at the next full moon, but we were not taking chances.

The place turned into an armed camp with everyone well-equipped. The next few weeks inched by with us continually making plans for different situations that might came at us. We felt ready when the full moon came around again. No one slept much, and we were all nervous. The moon came and went with no John Doe. On the first dark night, we started to relax somewhat. The next morning, I was walking toward the corrals when I heard a commotion at JL's cabin. Uncle Dockie, Aunt Marsha and a few others were milling about, so I trotted over. Aunt Marsha was more upset than I had ever seen her. Winston and Eric Alan were raging mad. I pushed my way in to find JL holding little Nine.

"JL, what is wrong?"

She pulled the blanket from the baby and there was a cross on his forehead drawn in blood. This was the most bone chilling moment of my life.

"Lord o'mercy, how did that get there?"

"I woke up to a terrible stench, and I went to check on Nine. There he was with that drawn on his forehead. At the foot of the bed was a bloody, dirty shirt. Pa says it was the shirt he killed and buried Snakebite in. Someone came in here last night and did this. He got past us and out again without us knowing." She just looked at me with wide eyes.

I walked outside to find Uncle Dockie. "Uncle Dockie, what do you think?"

"We got shown last night that our defenses are

useless. This had to be a John Doe trick. No-one other than him could do something like this. He is as sick and mean as any I have ever seen. He could have done worse, but only did this. I am confused as to what he is telling us."

Everyone was so upset that Aunt Marsha took over. "Everyone, listen up. We have a meeting in an hour at the house." She then walked away.

I got my horse and rode to where we buried Snakebite. All I found was an empty hole. John Doe must have dug up Snakebite's body and taken it. What he did with it was more than I wanted to imagine.

Chapter 29
Uncle Tucson

People were trying to get back to what they were doing, but the fearful energy was sky high. An hour later, we were in the house. Uncle Dockie had just stood up to talk when the door opened and in walked Tucson Slim. I had only met him once a few years ago when we all went down to Tucson for Uncle Dockie's murder trial. I had not seen him since.

He was an impressive looking man. Tall and slim. Long white hair with a deep tan. Good features. Still had all his teeth, white and perfect. Dressed with a look of success. He had no gun on his hip but a shoulder holster under his vest. The most striking thing about him is his deep blue eyes. It's as if he could see what you were thinking. Everyone stopped to see who came in. Uncle Dockie was very glad to see him. It was as if a big relief came over the room. Those who knew him were damn glad he was here.

After the welcome Uncle Dockie explained, "For those of you who don't know, this is my old friend, Tucson Slim. Tucson, we are damn glad to see you."

Tucson said, "I got your telegram that you were having trouble and I wanted to help. What can I do?"

JL asked, "Uncle Tucson, have you ever run across an outlaw called John Doe?"

His eyebrows went straight up. "Yes, I have. I chased him from time to time for the last twelve years but with no luck. Got real close a time or two. My only ambition in life is to kill him. Why?"

JL related the story to him as he listened patiently.

Then he said confidently, "It's time to finish my business with him. I will start tomorrow morning. Here is what you need to know. He loves to torture people with fear. When he tires of that, he will try to finish the grudge. In the meantime, I have a window of opportunity to get him. My guess is that he has gone back across the border. He knows you are on constant guard. He also knows that in time you will tire and start making mistakes. That's what he is waiting for. I plan to get this problem resolved."

Uncle Dockie asked, "How many people do you need, Tucson?"

He shook his head. "I don't want anyone with me. I work better alone."

We all left the meeting feeling better because Uncle Dockie seemed to look more at ease. There must have been a good reason for that. Aunt Marsha asked me to share my cabin with Tucson because all the beds were full. I walked Tucson down to my place. He had a pack horse with his gear, so we left it at my cabin and then took his animals to a pen. He spent the rest of the day at the main house getting caught up on this story. We all left them alone and tried to be useful around the place. That evening he came back and we sat in front of the fire. I didn't push, but I was curious.

I let him talk and at just the right moment I asked, "Tucson, I don't know anything about you. I'm dying to ask but don't want to be rude."

He just looked at me and smiled. Then he said, "My first years were much the same as the other boys. I was born in a whore house in Tucson. I remember my ma some. I thought she was wonderful. As I got older, I realized just how wonderful. She made a living for us the only way she could in those hard times. Most whores are drunks or have Chinese drug problems, but she didn't. She was just surviving.

"I was probably around ten years old when a drunk man used her and then killed her for asking to be paid. This was the start of bad times getting worse. I walked in as he was leaving, so I knew who he was. I told the sheriff, but his response was, 'Let it go, kid. She was only a whore.' This was a crushing blow to me.

"When I was through crying in a back alley, I decided to take care of things myself. I waited outside his favorite saloon. He staggered out drunk, heading to where he lived. I had a knife like all little boys. I walked up to him and ran it in his heart. Down he went, and I was off running before anybody saw me. At least I thought so. The sheriff found me the next day and hauled me into the sheriff's office. Truth is he didn't know what to do with me. I was only ten, maybe eleven years old.

"The local law decided to send me to a boys' reform school back east in Ohio. I got shipped back there and life got hard. Real hard. It was like prison for teenagers, but I wasn't even a teenager yet. The place was a living hell for me. It was either get tough and fight back or die, so I fought back. I was getting beat up every day because I was younger than most of them, but over time, I learned a trick or two. Whoever beat me up would get a surprise visit in the dark of night. I used chairs or anything hard to crack their head. This kept on until people learned I was a sneak attack kind of guy and I was willing to go as long as they were. Eventually they started leaving me be. I was there for three years and they decided I was not reformable. They talked about an adult prison for me, so I made serious plans to escape."

Uncle Tucson continued with his story…

The Break Out

It was much easier than I thought it might be. The delivery wagons came and went real regular. I just slipped inside a garbage wagon and out I went. I hid out by day and ran by night. I stole clothes and food enough to stay alive. I was heading west where I wanted to be and just knew life would be better. I made it to St. Joseph, Missouri. That was a place that wagon trains left from going west, so that was just the place for me. A family of pilgrims felt sorry for me and took me in. The woman was nice but the man a religious idiot. We were on the Santa Fe Trail and close to Santa Fe when I decided it was time to jump ship. Hell, he didn't care, so off I went to Santa Fe. Life was no easier for me there. I was a street orphan and white. The local Mex population didn't fall in love with me. My luck changed when I found a band of young outlaws that understood my desperate situation. The leader was a kid named Pox. He was a little older then I was.

One say, he walked up to me and said, "You white?"

"Yup," I said.

The young tough looked at me. "You tired of being poor and shit on?"

By that time, I was as tough as they come. "Do I look happy with my condition?"

He smiled at my comeback. "What be your name?"

"They call me Tucson Slim. What be yours?"

"Pox. I had the pox but lived through the problem. I got the scars to prove it."

I was so desperate I would have made a deal with anyone at that time. "What you got to offer me?" I said.

"Just throw in with us, and I'll show you how to get along in this world."

C-Bar

"I ain't got no horse, gun or clothes. Won't be much help."

Ol' Pox just laughed. "You will by tomorrow."

That night we snuck into a stable and stole a horse and saddle. Next night we broke into a general store and got me the clothes and gun that I needed. I was real happy with myself. I looked good, had some money from the general store and was eating real food.

There were six of us in all. We stole everything we could find. Broke into every unguarded house and carried off everything we could carry. We stole cattle, but eventually we graduated to banks. Cattle had to be stolen and then run to a buyer. Very labor intensive. The banks bypassed all that. We just did a bank holdup and had the money a lot quicker. It all was working real good until the law got real serious and wanted to hang us. Now the pressure was on. We were on the run day and night. Our crew was dwindling down. Some were caught and hanged. Some shot out of their saddles. I sat with Pox in a dry wash one evening in the dark.

"Pox, ol' boy, we are in a world of hurt here. I do believe it's time to head to Arizona. They don't know us there."

"Well, Tucson, what we going to do in Arizona?"

All I could say was the truth. "Maybe stay alive."

He agreed and off we went. Amazes me to this day that we got there alive. Me and ol' Pox were running for our lives. Hiding by day and traveling by night. The law was always not far behind. They had an Injun tracker, and nothing we did was enough to lose them. I made a decision.

"Pox, our only hope is to outrun them. I'm willing to hit every pilgrim's place for food and fresh horses. The law won't do that. What do you think?"

He agreed, so at night we would look for house lights. The first one we saw, we roared into, scaring the people to death. I felt terrible about it, but desperate people do desperate deeds.

The pilgrims were all huddled in a corner of the cabin. I said, "We don't want to hurt you. Please don't make us. All we need is food and fresh horses. If we don't get them we are dead men."

The man stood up and looked less afraid. "I understand, boys. We will feed you and give you two horses. When you find new ones, just let our horses go and they will come home. Does that work for you?"

With huge relief, I responded, "Yes, sir. That is all we want."

An hour later, we were off and going again. Food in our bellies and fresh horses under us. We actually got some distance made from the posse with this new tactic. The next cabin didn't go so well. They were poor, had nothing, and were barely feeding themselves. We still took what they had and ran. I feel bad about doing that to this very day. In fact, years later, I went back there hoping to find a successful homestead operating. Found nothing but burned timbers. That is something that will haunt me for the rest of my days. Anyway, this idea worked, and we outran the posse. When we rode into Arizona, we were broke, hungry and desperate again. All we knew was stealing and only thing to steal was cattle. A big lesson was learned about robbing banks in New Mexico. It seemed to us that a few missing cattle wouldn't be noticed. We were wrong. People were after us again. Weren't no law here. Just ranchers willing to hang a cattle thief real quick. Ol' Pox was losing his resolve to stay alive. I watched him get quieter and quieter. Just didn't seem to care anymore.

The local ranchers were closing in when he looked at me and said, "Tucson, keep running. I'm, however, through with that. I've been running my whole life, hoping to stay alive. My running is over."

He turned and went at them. I ran the other direction but could hear the gunshots. I knew they killed him. It did give me the time I needed to get shed of the people chasing me. I will always feel fondly for ol' Pox. He found and befriended me when I didn't have a friend in the world. I still love him.

Fred and Hazel Barnett

I was close to my old stomping grounds. The town of Tucson was just ahead. I was really down and out now, starving and close to my end. I passed out and fell off my horse. When I woke up, I was being held by an old man. He was pouring water down my throat. I passed out again to wake up in a bed.

An older woman was fixing a meal and it smelled like heaven to me. I tried to get up when she walked over to me and sat on the bed. "Young man," she said, "you need to rest. Stay in that bed."

All I could say was, "Ma'am, I'm hungry. Can I eat something, please?"

She smiled ear to ear, looked at the man who found me and said, "He'll be fine, Fred. Let's get him to the table."

They helped me up and sat me down in front of the best meal I ever ate. I can't remember what it was, but it was the best food of my life.

The C-Bar

Fred and Hazel took me in like family, and I needed family real bad. I wasn't the only one they adopted. There was Philo Sundeen, NoName Smith, Bobby Blue and Buck Bailey. We were all kids abandoned early and taken in by the Barnetts. They believed that love and kindness is all a child needs. They poured it on us and we responded. We would have done anything for those people. The bond between us boys was as strong as brothers. We all needed this family and didn't take it for granted. Being alone in a hard world makes one appreciate a family.

The days were filled with work and that is just what young boys need. Fred was patient with us and always took the time to talk about any problems. Every now and then, he had to break up a squabble, but none of us could bear the thought of making him or Hazel unhappy.

Hazel became our mother. She fussed over us constantly. She made sure we were fed, clean and well dressed. Every one of us loved the attention. When you find something you haven't had, it's lifesaving. If Hazel looked unhappy, the guilty party caught hell from the rest and got straight real quick.

***

At this point, I interrupted the story and asked, "Tucson, when did Uncle Dockie come in to the family?"

"Ah, well," he began, "we were all teenagers about that time. Fred and Buck were out and attacked by Apaches. Fred was wounded and couldn't ride, so he sent Buck to get us. When Buck made a break, most of the Apache went after him. They left two behind to close in on Fred. At the last minute, Dockie came to his rescue. Killed both the Apache warriors with a rock. Got Fred bandaged up. That's how he got his name. When we got back, Fred was with this kid who was dressed like a Mexican. Skinny and ragged looking. We understood about being down and out, so he was adopted right on the spot.

"Dockie brought something to our family that is hard to describe. He was strong but not a hard person. There's no anger in him, which the rest of us had to deal with. He actually cared about people and animals. Natural born leader. His judgement was always good. He floated to the top of our group when it came to making decisions. We all loved him and learned a great deal from Dockie."

I still had more questions. "Tucson, I know some about your leaving southern Arizona, but what is your memory of coming here?"

He got serious with this answer.

"We were all young and full of mischief. Going to town every payday was great fun. We fought and gambled our money away with the townsfolk. Then one day, Hazel started getting sick. A few days later, she passed away, and we were all crushed. I still tear up thinking about that." Tucson took out a handkerchief and blew his nose. I looked away.

After he composed himself, he continued, "Life just went downhill bad at that time. Come payday, we went to town again. Fred and Dockie tried to stop us but we were all so mad at the world, nothing was going to stop us. That trip we weren't the fun-loving bunch of kids we normally were. We were getting drunk and mean when a local tough started in on us."

Tucson then looked at me and with remorse in his face and voice, and said, "I was the one that killed him. Everyone knew it was me, but no-one ever said a word about it. Now the law was after us. Fred got us together and said we were leaving. 'Gather up the herd. We were are going north.' What Dockie did then is why we all are so devoted to him. He waited until dark, went to town and surprised the sheriff. Held a gun on him and told the man he was the one that killed the town boy. That he was leaving and going south. This let us have time to finish the roundup. He didn't go south but circled the herd for several days. We had some bounty hunter trouble, but Dockie took care of that problem. We ended up here."

He seemed to need a break, so I made coffee. I was enjoying this and sure hoped he wouldn't stop. I wasn't disappointed.

"Chris, I have never told this story to anyone. Am I boring you?"

"Hell, no, you ain't boring me. I would be very disappointed if you didn't finish the story."

Tucson looked relieved and launched into the remainder of his tale…

***

We settled in here and started the ranch. Problem I had is that I just didn't like being a cowboy. Being a cowboy in town on Saturday night is one thing, but being a cowboy on Monday morning is a different thing altogether. Truthfully, I was screaming bored. Now, don't laugh, but I always wanted to be a Texas Ranger. I had all I could stand one day and announced that I was leaving to explore the world. I wasn't the only one feeling that way, so it was accepted easily by everyone. So off I went to Texas.

The Rangers

I arrived in Austin on a Monday and was a sworn in Ranger on Tuesday. They needed help so bad, the interview process was easy. I asked around and found the headquarters and walked in.

A man behind the desk looked up and said, "What you need, boy?"

"I came from Arizona to be a Ranger. Any chance of that happening?"

The older man sat back in his chair looking me over. "Why?"

I just told him the truth. "Don't really know. Just always wanted to be a Texas Ranger."

C-Bar

He didn't respond; was just thinking and looking me over. "You wanted for anything?"

"No."

"You are carrying a gun. Do you have a horse?"

"Yes, I do, and a damn fine one."

"Put your right hand in the air."

He swore me in then and there, and I was a Texas Ranger. I was young and didn't know that anything this easy to get into probably had some drawbacks.

The man asked, "What's your name, boy?"

"Tucson Slim, sir."

He scribbled my name on a piece of paper and shoved it over to me. "Can you sign your name?" he asked.

"Yes, I can," I said proudly, but only because of Hazel making us learn the basics. She thought we should be able to sign our names. Truth is that's all I can do even to this day. So, I signed the paper and looked at the man.

"Well, boy," he said, "your dreams have come true. Go out the door, turn left and follow the road to the Ranger camp. Can't miss it. Tell them you are a new recruit."

And I did just that. Walked to a grove of oak trees and there were twenty or so cabin tents. I asked who was in charge and was pointed to a man sitting at a fire drinking coffee. I walked over to him. "I was told to come here and tell you I am a new Ranger."

The man looked up, and before he said a word, another man rushed to the fella I was talking to.

"Captain, Comanch raid six miles north. Two homes burned and horses stolen. Heading west."

The captain stood up and barked, "Get ready, boys."

The camp came alive with men getting trail ready. The captain looked at me and said, "Get on your horse, boy. We are about to find out what you are made of."

Eight of us rolled out of camp at a long trot, heading west-by-northwest. I assumed we went this way to cut off the raiding party heading west to their place of safety. Two hours later, the captain came to a sudden stop.

He turned to us and barked again, "That dust ahead is going to be them, boys. Let's give them hell!"

We left at a dead run and a few minutes later slammed right into them. The fight was on. After a few minutes, we had killed two of them, and I am sure wounded more. One of our men was dead and another wounded. Me and two more got the duty of returning the livestock while the others took our dead and wounded back to camp. That was my first day of service for the Texas Rangers. I did pretty much the same thing for the next two years. I was either chasing Comanche or outlaws.

That was the first time I encountered John Doe. He is a murderous bastard who terrorized Texas. I saw his destruction many times. We could never get close to him. He's insane but smart. Never even laid eyes on him. I always regretted that. Being a Ranger was my life until suddenly things changed.

Bonnie Joe McCoy

I had learned and proven myself to be a good Ranger. No-one questioned my courage. Then one day in town I walked into the general store. I looked over and saw a woman buying something or another. I was struck by her. Not what most would call a beautiful woman. She didn't have fine features and a small, slim frame. But when she looked at me, she smiled. Her nature was that of a happy and confident woman. I then did the bravest thing I have ever done. I walked up to her.

"Hello, miss. My name be Tucson Slim. Can I ask what your name be?"

She looked at me and smiled. "Hello, Mr. Slim. My name is Bonnie Joe McCoy. How are you this fine day?"

I was amazed that she actually talked to me. "Is there any chance in the world that you would let me buy you a cup of coffee?"

"That sounds wonderful, Mr. Slim. When?"

I just looked at her in disbelief. "Um… now?"

"That would be just fine."

She stuck out her elbow for me to take, and I escorted her across the street to a cafe. We hit it off immediately. Why she liked me is not understandable, but why I liked her was plain to see. Her nature was happy. She smiled most of the time. I saw kindness and concern in her face. Now that I'm telling this story, I am thinking that she reminds me of Hazel. Don't really matter—I was in love.

We was married for fifteen years. Best time of my life. I loved her dearly. I used to just sit and watch her go about her business. When she caught me doing that she just smiled.

***

I was leaning forward, intent on every word. "So, what happened, Tucson?"

He explained, "I gave up being a Ranger and went to work in a blacksmith shop. That was a hard day to wake up to in the morning, so I went to being a local deputy. Weren't hard work. A drunk in town now and then.

C-Bar

Nothing dangerous. The pay weren't very good, but I got to stay in town and visit with people most of the day. Bonnie Joe had a dress shop, so I visited with her a lot.

"Then it all went bad. There was a bank robbery. On the way out of town, the gang was shooting at anything that walked. Bonnie was in her shop making a dress when she was hit by a bullet. They killed her. My life was over at that moment. After the grief came the anger. One of the gang was wounded and we captured him. Man said he was part of the John Doe gang.

"I sold everything I had and set out to kill him. He is a wily and elusive bastard. When I ran out of money, I had to take a job to survive. Went to work for Wells Fargo. I like the way they operate. When they have a problem, they don't worry about the law. They just want solutions. Fargo would just send me out to find the guilty riff-raff and end the problem. This job let me continually try to find John Doe. I have twelve years with Wells Fargo now.

"I got a telegram from Dockie saying they needed me, so I came, never suspecting it was a problem with John Doe. Persistence and luck go hand in hand. Over time, I figured out that to penetrate a gang's confidence I needed an alias, so Wells Fargo cooked up the alias of Canyon Red."

I was surprised. "You don't mean to tell me you are the notorious Canyon Red?"

He chuckled, clearly amused. "Yup, that's me. Wells Fargo keeps putting out false wanted posters on me. Tomorrow when I leave I will be Canyon Red."

Early the next morning, Tucson left looking much different than when he came. His clothes were dirty and well worn. Looked like a man who slept on the trail. He was carrying two pistols in shoulder holsters. In his boot was a wanted poster for Canyon Red—wanted for murder and bank robbery. He looked the part.

C-Bar

Chapter 30
Tucson Returns

Ten days after Tucson left, he returned late one day. He looked like hell. He was leading a horse upon which sat a man in chains. The man was small and had the look of a caged tiger. His eyes were darting in every direction. Dockie came out of the house to see what was drawing the crowd.

Tucson said, "This be John Doe. I brought him back alive so everyone could see him as just a man and nothing special. He lives to create fear in people. I don't want anyone here to be afraid of this pathetic excuse for a human being. Tomorrow he meets his maker, but for now I need to rest."

Tucson needed help getting off his horse so Uncle Dockie and I helped him down. He then handed Uncle Dockie the key to the shackles.

Uncle Dockie turned to Big Mike and said, "Mike, would you chain John Doe to a tree for us?"

Mike stepped forward and Uncle Dockie handed him the key. He then (not so gently) pulled John Doe from his horse and dragged him off.

Tucson looked at me, exhaustion written all over him. "Chris, I need a bath and a bed. Can I stay with you tonight?"

I just smiled and nodded my head. Tucson was weak from his ordeal, so Uncle Dockie and I helped him to my cabin. We more carried then helped. When inside, Uncle Dockie sat him down and started to get him undressed. I fired up the water heater and got a hot bath going. The water was nearly to the top of the tub, so we helped Tucson get in. When up to his neck, he was melting away. We let him soak for a good ten minutes. Then I washed his body while Uncle Dockie washed his hair. When we had him clean and dry, he was put in my extra bed. Asleep is not a good enough word for what he was doing.

The next day I saw his eyes fluttering. I had been keeping an eye on him, so I walked over to his bed.

"How you feeling, Tucson?"

"A bath, good bed and twelve hours of sleep have done wonders for me. Thanks, Chris."

He got up but was stiff and sore. Thirty minutes later, he was shaved and dressed in the clothes he arrived in and looked damn good. For the shape he was in the day before, he sure had recovered.

"Tucson, you hungry?" I asked.

"Dockie used to say he was hungry enough to eat the ass out of a buffalo. I completely understand that statement now."

We walked down to the cook shack but were told by Frying Pan Charlie, "Miss Marsha says she wants to feed you at the house."

So we walked that way. When we walked in Aunt Marsha came over and gave Tucson a big kiss and a hug. Tucson enjoyed that a lot.

She put his face in her hands and cooed, "Tucson, you are still a handsome devil. Thank you for coming. Sit down. I have breakfast almost ready."

Aunt Marsha must have seen us coming because food was put in front of us as soon as we sat down. We ate everything on our plates and drank a lot of coffee. Mostly chatted, just small talk about the grandchildren.

When we were done, Uncle Dockie patted Tucson's arm and asked, "So, can you tell us what happened?"

"Sure, I can."

C-Bar

Chapter 31
Naco, Mexico

Uncle Tucson related the whole story of how he tracked down the evil John Doe...

I had my first good lead on John Doe in the last twelve years. An old score needed to be settled, and I was driven to get close enough to Doe to kill him. I left the ranch and headed south to Mexico. I was three hard days getting there. Looking like an outlaw ain't hard to do when you do a long trip like that. I had never been to Naco before, but this town was a typical outlaw hideout. People are dirt poor. No law to protect them. The Mexican government is too far away to send help. The John Doe gang had complete control. I was a quarter-mile out when I came to a gruesome site. On the side of the road were three dead men hanging on crosses. The first was an old vaquero-looking kind of man. Had the clothes that you will see them wear. Probably sixty years old. The second was a typical town type of man and the third was of a man long dead. Had no shirt on. It was a hideous sight.

I went to the stable but found no one watching the place, so I put my horse in a stall and threw him some hay. It was plain to see where the cantina was so I walked in. I bellied up to the bar. Bartender came over looking at me over real hard.

I looked back. "Bartender, I want a beer, and I don't want your eyes on me."

C-Bar

He looked away real fast and shortly returned with the beer. He tried to be nice. "Come a long way, mister?"

I nodded my head. "A long way, for sure."

I think the bartender was looking for information as to who I was, as he tried to get a conversation going. "Anything you need I will be glad to send you in the right direction. This place is the hub of Naco."

I took advantage of the offer. "What the hell is up with crucifying people and putting them on display?"

The bartender got nervous. "One was an old vaquero that had loose lips, and the other was the stable owner that John Doe lost faith in."

I was gettin' curious. "What about the third one?"

The bartender walked away real quick. From behind me, I heard this: "The third is the one betrayed by the other two. Like Jesus and the people who betrayed him."

I turned to see a smaller man with wild eyes. I figured him for John Doe.

"Well, I'm new in town, but I'm learning fast that there are some not to get on the wrong side of in this town."

This crazy-looking man was looking me up and

down. "Getting on the wrong side of people here can be a bad idea. Who are you and why are you in town?"

"Mister, I'm just looking for a friendlier place to be and find a man called John Doe. Know him?"

This really got his attention. "What you want with him?"

"Word is he is looking for help with a personal problem. I'm good help with that sort of thing."

"Just how did you hear that?"

"In my world, a lot of information gets spread around. Do you know him?"

He was looking me over real hard. This type never trusts anyone and with good reason. Everyone in his world is an outlaw.

"Yeah, I know him. I'm John Doe."

I responded as if I were surprised. "Well, that was easy. Do you need help or did I ride down here for nothing?"

This crazy bastard was either going to kill me or take me in. It could have gone either way. He nodded his head toward a table of hard cases. I followed him and sat down at the table.

"Boys, this here fella wants to join us. Anyone know him?"

I was sweating this out. However, no one said they'd run into me before. This was pure luck.

One of them spoke up. "My name is Paul Thomas. Ever heard of me?"

"Yes… I have heard your name. Aren't you a Sunday school teacher?"

My little joke fell flat. They all froze up and looked at John Doe. His eyes were getting bigger. "Me and my followers don't joke about things like that. We are all God-fearing people. Don't make that mistake again."

I was on the edge right then, so I decided to just shut up.

Doe looked at me again. "What they call you?"

"They call me Red. Canyon Red."

If they were going to kill me, it was right then. They all knew the name. Doe's eyes squinted. "Can you prove that?"

I reached for my boot and several pistols were in my face. So I moved real slow and pulled out my wanted poster. They looked it over and compared me to the drawn picture. It seemed to satisfy them. They put their guns away. The drinking started then. All the hired guns had bought my story and were impressed with me. John Doe wasn't won over yet.

"Get to know everyone. We'll talk tomorrow."

Where he went I don't know, but he left with a purpose. I felt like he had an information source he was checking me out with but then, hell, I didn't know anything for sure at this point in time. I just kept drinking with this outlaw trash and trying to pick up any information I could. It's a tricky business asking questions. Do it wrong and you trigger suspicion. There was one man I was feeling was a little different than most of them. He didn't seem to fit the low class he was running with. I was trying to get some conversation going his way.

"Hey, pard, what should I call you?"

"I go by Smith."

"Well, Smith, how you come to be south of the border?"

He didn't seem to be concerned with my question. "Pulled an ignorant stunt that went wrong and now I'm here."

I looked at him with concern. "Let me tell you, Smith, you are looking at the man who has done every stunt wrong at least twice. Whatever you did, I can top."

He took the bait. He said, "I was a young teenager and thought robbing a bank would be fun and easy money. It went wrong when the teller pulled a gun and I shot him. My life ended that day."

This young fella was not here by choice. He was driven to this depraved place because he had nowhere else to go. He was the one for me to work on.

"Well, young fella, let's you and me find some shade and you tell me what your future plans are."

He replied, "My plans in life are probably rotting in hell. It is getting hot, so I'm up for some shade."

We walked over to a tree and sat on a bench.

"Smith, have you been with this bunch for long?"

"Nope, just a week or so. Waiting for the next run north."

This kid had no idea what was in store for him. I felt safe enough to start asking questions. "Tell me about John Doe. He scares me some."

"He scares me too, Red. Did you see the crosses outside of town? I think he's as crazy as they come. The one in the middle is his son. They call him Snakebite. If I had any options, I would be gone. Red, why you here?"

"Like you, Smith, got nowhere else to go. I'm as desperate as you are."

This boy was not mean or an outlaw. I felt sorry for him. The evening came and went. The drunkenness just got worse. The riff-raff were starting to fight among themselves. I drifted away and went to my horse. I slept in the stall with him. I didn't sleep worth a damn, but I was thinking no one would suspect me of sleeping here in horse shit and piss.

The next day I was up and wandered down to the cantina. Everyone was there except Smith. I didn't inquire. John Doe showed up and was in a rage.

"Smith done lit out. The traitor needs to find God's judgement today. Let's go, boys."

Everyone headed for the horses. We were up and going within thirty minutes. One of them cut his trail pretty quick so we knew which direction he was going. We set out in a long trot. Became evident soon that the boy wasn't trying to cover his trail. Probably thought he could just walk away. We tore after him and soon had him in sight. He turned to look behind himself. Smith just sat there watching us get closer until he must have finally figured it out. He turned and ran.

We were close but our horses were a little bit more wore down. Smith managed to keep out of rifle distance. Then he made a mistake. Smith slowed down and let us get a little too close. John Doe made a quick stop, dismounted and pulled his rifle. Either he is a great marksman or lucky—I don't know—but he fired and down Smith and his horse went. We were on him quick after that. John Doe was screaming and ranting at the boy. I thought he would probably kill him, but he threw Smith up behind another rider and we headed for town.

I was thinking he would make a big deal about killing the boy, but I had no idea what he was going to do. We rode to the place just outside of town where he had crucified the three people. He rode a short distance away and came back, dragging another cross. I was about to get sick, watching them tie his feet and wrists to the cross. When he was tied, they drove long nails in his hands and feet. They then cut the ropes and pulled the cross up and into a post hole. His weight was now hanging on his nailed hands. The boy was screaming. I just couldn't watch, so I pulled my pistol and shot Smith through the heart. He was dead instantly. John Doe turned to look at me with rage in his heart. He turned and walked toward me.

"Why did you let him out that easy!!"

I have no idea why I said what I did, but it was the right thing to say. I stated, "God told me to do it."

He stopped in his tracks and stared at me.

"God told me Satan was waiting impatiently and to hurry up."

I knew now that I was either going to die or he might just buy what I said. I'll be going to Hell, but he just turned and walked away. I actually think he bought it.

That evening the drinking started again. Same as before. John Doe walked out of the shadows, dragging a little girl maybe ten years old. Everyone stopped to see what he had in mind. Doe waited until he had everyone's attention.

He said, "I have a gift for our newest follower. This little virgin needs to become a whore tonight, and she is Red's for the taking."

My mind started racing. This man was as smart as I have ever seen. He was testing me. Was I the type to take this little girl or find some way out? That would tell him about me, and I would live or die with my next move.

I jumped up and grabbed her away from him. I started dragging her to an empty house just outside the cantina walls. I dragged her in and slammed the door. I looked around and found a bedroom. Thank God it had no windows. I sat her on the bed. She was sobbing and my heart was being torn out just watching. I truthfully didn't know what to do. Then I had my answer.

She said, "Please, don't hurt me."

Much to my relief this little girl could speak English. I whispered to her, "Don't worry, sweetheart. I won't hurt you."

I repeated this several times, and she finally started to calm down. I was wiping her tears from her cheek. She must have believed me because she laid her head on my chest and sobbed. I wanted to cry myself.

I whispered to her again, "What is your name, sweetheart?"

She looked at me. "Juanita."

"Juanita, can you play a game with me?"

She nodded her head.

"When we leave here, you must hold your head down as if you are in trouble with your mama. Can you do that?"

She nodded her head. I waited for a while and then walked out of the house with the little girl. I had her by the arm and entered the cantina. I looked at the men at the table.

"This is my woman now. Any man who touches her I will kill. Do you understand?"

No-one said a word. Then John Doe walked out of the shadows and asked, "Just why do you think she is yours?"

I figured I would try this one more time. "Because

God married us in that house. She is my wife in the eyes of God now."

The crazy son of a bitch accepted that again. I had found his weakness. He walked over to the table and said to the gathered men, "We are enough to get to work tomorrow. I plan to raid a rich ranch. We will kill all the men and carry off the gold and women. This will make us all rich. Be ready by sunup."

Then he walked away. I took the little girl and returned to the empty house. We sat and just looked at each other. I took her to make sure she was not harmed for at least this night. I said, "Juanita, do you live with your mama?"

She sadly shook her head no. "My mama was shot a short time ago."

Chris had told me about what happened to him down here.

"Was your mama Annabelle?"

Her eyes teared up. I knew the story now.

"Juanita, do you have any family?"

Again, she shook her head. Broke my heart. That night this scared and lonely little girl slept on my lap. The following early morning I took her to a church. The priest was long gone but there was a woman praying at the altar. I interrupted her.

"Excuse me, ma'am. Can we talk?"

She stood and looked at me. There was the blank look of someone who didn't know English. All I could do was reach for her hand and place it on Juanita's shoulder. I then gave her twenty dollars. She understood. I had done all I could do, so I left and found everyone getting ready for the raid.

There was John Doe, nine of his cutthroats, and myself heading north. We didn't hurry. Just kept up a steady pace. That evening John Doe had brought us to an abandoned cabin. It was small—everyone couldn't sleep inside, so four of us were sleeping outside. At midnight I knew I had to do something but had no idea of what. The answer came soon.

John Doe walked out to relieve himself. He stepped away from the door. I didn't even think. I jumped up and knocked him cold with my gun barrel. Down he went. I then went over to the campfire and picked up my rifle. All three were sleeping soundly. They had been drinking whiskey so they were out cold. One at a time, I straddled them and crushed their heads with my rifle butt. There was only the sound of breaking bones. No one stirred in the cabin. Ten minutes later, I had John Doe tied to his horse and mine saddled. I had a set of handcuffs in a saddlebag, so I ran one side under the pommel where the saddle horn is attached. Doe had a wrist on either side and was going nowhere. I slowly left camp and when out of hearing range mounted up and left at a long trot.

At sunup we had covered ground, but I wasn't slowing down. Doe had come-to and was ranting like the crazy man he is. To think that the gang wouldn't come after us was only hopeful thinking. I could tell they were behind us because of the dust cloud. Wasn't much hope of outrunning them, so thinning down the crowd was my only hope. We turned a sharp corner in the road so I pulled over. Doe was not shutting up, so I thumped his head again and tied up the horses. It was then easy to lay in wait. They came around the corner, and I must say, a little foolishly with no caution. Might have been the whiskey hangover.

They were fifty feet away when I started shooting. Three went down and the rest scattered. The only thing to do now was run like hell and hope they had learned enough to not follow. This crew don't learn too quick.

John Doe is a lunatic, but he must garner support for some reason because they kept coming, however, a little more carefully. They kept the pressure on me for the remainder of the day. I had to do something, so I laid another trap.

It's hard to travel at night. Everyone holes up and tries to get some rest for the next day. This gave me an opportunity. It was dark. A smart person will just do a dry camp. No fire or smoke to give themselves away. Getting downwind is a good way to smell smoke and follow it to the fire. I got the faintest whiff of smoke, telling me they had a small fire in the hope of not being seen. The need for coffee probably outweighed their common sense. It was easy to get close enough to see them huddled around the fire getting warm and drinking coffee. They were probably planning their next move. My Winchester had twelve rounds in the magazine. It made sense to just let loose. I could see two go down immediately. The rest scattered, so I emptied the rifle in the general direction. Everything went quiet, so I hightailed it back to Doe and the horses. He wasn't happy about being thrown on a horse again but who cares? So off we went.

The next day about noon, Doe and I were on a hilltop waiting to see if there were any more following us. There were two. It's amazing to me how someone like John Doe can get such a loyal following. I don't think I could have killed or wounded that many last night to only leave two. Maybe some were wounded or finally came to their senses. I don't know, but it was time to finish this. After two nights of no sleep, no food and no water, I was not thinking like I normally would. Ol' John was not happy about being chained to a thorn tree, but it was a fun thing for me to do.

I mounted up and worked my way down the hill. The two remaining idiots came into sight when I rushed them from a dry wash. One was blown out of his saddle and the other ran. However, that one made a big mistake. He ran up a hill, which slowed him down considerably. The downed outlaw had a Winchester on his horse, so it was easy to get in my hands. On the third shot, blood came flying out of the man's shoulder about where the collarbone is. I knew if he didn't die out there, he would at least not follow. From there on, it was a clear ride to the ranch.

C-Bar

Chapter 32
John Doe Meets His End

After Tucson told what happened, we got up and walked to where John Doe was chained to a tree. Big Mike had sat there all night to make sure he didn't escape.

Big Mike just shook his head when he saw us approaching. "This man has been ranting and raving all night. I have seen crazy, but never mean-crazy like this."

Tucson looked at Uncle Dockie and myself. "I'm going to dispose of this trash. Do you boys want to give me a hand?"

We saddled four horses, unchained John Doe from the tree, and dragged him over to the horse. We rode away from the ranch. We were not talking, just riding, when Tucson spoke.

"I don't want this man buried on the C-Bar. I saw some worthless ground that no-one would have any reason to go to. He needs to just disappear from the world."

We rode off the ranch to a sandy and isolated place — a very lonely part of the world. John Doe never shut up, ranting religious gibberish. He was quoting the Bible and screaming nonsense in general. Tucson dismounted so we did also. He pulled John Doe from his horse and sat him on the ground. He just looked at the crazy man and finally deciding he wouldn't shut up, he put a gag in his mouth.

Then he got in John Doe's face. "Did losing your son pain you?"

John Doe just tried to rant through the gag. Tucson stepped back and shot him in the knee. Doe was trying to scream but wouldn't quit his rant. Tucson stepped back again and shot him in the other knee. This made him scream in pain, but he finally quit the ranting. The pain seemed to get his attention.

Tucson got close to his face again and repeated slowly, "Did losing your son cause you pain?"

John Doe slowly blinked his eyes and a moment later nodded his head.

"When you killed my wife, I felt the same pain," Tucson said.

You never know what someone is thinking, but I could swear that John Doe's eyes had the expression of someone understanding something for the first time. He put down his head and tears started flowing. Tucson stood up, pulled his pistol and shot John Doe in the head.

Uncle Dockie then commented, "I vote that we let the animals eat him. He don't deserve a resting place."

Nothing more was said. We just got on our horses and headed home.

A few minutes later, Uncle Dockie asked Tucson, "What plans you have now?"

Tucson pondered for a moment and then responded, "Thought maybe I would stay on the ranch for a spell. Sitting on your porch in the sun sounds like a nice place to be."

Uncle Dockie moved his horse over near Tucson and rubbed his back, saying, "Ain't my porch, Tucson. It's our porch."

I was glad to be riding in the back because this made me tear up. I think Tucson had found his way home again.

C-Bar

Chapter 33
The Cleanup

Three days of sitting on the porch gave Tucson a new lease on life. He asked Uncle Dockie, JL and myself if he could talk with us. Of course, we agreed. We all met on the porch.

He informed us, "I am going back to Naco. There may be a few leftovers who made it back to the town alive. If so, that means we have people out there who could come back to haunt us. Won't be many, but even one could seek revenge."

Uncle Dockie responded, "When we leaving?"

Tucson looked relieved. "Tomorrow at sunup."

When the sun started to shine brightly we were already an hour down the trail. Looked like we were going to war again. Three days later, we were looking down on Naco. As we rode closer, things around town looked different. The people were in the fields working. The crosses outside the cantina were gone. Shops were open and busy. Someone recognized us, and the crowd gathered around. We were welcomed with open arms. I knew then that there were no remaining outlaws in town.

I asked and was told by a shop owner, "Three came back. They were looking poorly. We killed them with our farm tools."

There was a big party that evening. The cantina was now a happy place. It was decorated and lit up with lanterns. A band was playing and people were dancing. I was sitting with Uncle Dockie.

"Uncle Dockie, where is Tucson? I haven't seen him for a while."

Dockie shrugged. "I don't know, Chris. He's looking for someone, I guess."

Not long afterward, Tucson emerged out of the crowd and sat with us. I was about to ask what or who he was looking for when JL found us.

"Uncle Tucson, I have some news. John Doe killed a lot of village people and made a lot of children orphans. They are being fed in the church right now."

Tucson was up and gone. We followed behind. When we got to the church, Tucson led our way in. There were twenty or more small children inside. They all turned to see who came in. A little girl stood up and looked at us. Tucson saw her at the same time. They both ran toward each other. The little girl jumped into his arms. They were very glad to see each other. After a little loving, Tucson brought her over to us.

"Everyone, I want you to meet Juanita. I'm taking her home with me."

Mark Baugher

We all had something in our eyes at that moment. Damn dust, anyway.

C-Bar

Chapter 34
Back Home

When we all arrived home, it was a warm welcome for sure. Everyone soon knew that the nest of outlaws was no more. We just came from one party and we were right into another. There was a big bonfire that everyone gathered around. Clay and Ned were playing our favorite music. To have such a terrible experience be over and good times back was the most wonderful making for a celebration.

Uncle Dockie seemed to be over his depression concerning NoName. The world gave him a big load that had the best of him for a while. He was, however, a pioneer of this country and his type don't stay down long. Everyone in the family and extended family was in attendance. People were asking Tucson about Juanita.

"I fell in love with the little girl. We were both in trouble and clung to each other. Dockie says hard times make strong bonds. I believe that to be true."

The next day, life was getting back to normal. A lot of work had been neglected since we'd been forced into making an armed fort of the ranch for a time. However, no one complained. That evening we were all sitting at the supper table. Tucson had an announcement.

"Listen up! I have some news. Wells Fargo sent me a letter with a new job offer. They want me to be the superintendent of all the Wells Fargo business in

Arizona. My main office will be in Prescott. Juanita and I will live there. We will, however, be frequent visitors to the ranch."

We were all happy for Tucson. His previous line of work was putting him at risk, and he had Juanita to think about now. They both had each other and were holding on tight. The family took Juanita in like their own, but that is just what the Barnett clan does.

I made this comment at the table: "I just want everything to get back to normal. Peaceful and quiet. Is that too much to ask?"

Little Dez piped up, saying, "Papa says it's always something, Chris. I don't know what that means, but 'it's always something' is what he says."

This brought a big round of laughter. From the mouth of babes will come the truth. All right, then… Was it too much to ask for a little breather before the next big adventure?

Chapter 35
The Mystery Woman

We started noticing unusual happenings on the ranch. Every now and then, Uncle Dockie would be seen talking with a woman who no-one recognized. When they were approached, the woman would fade away. Uncle Dockie was very closed-mouthed about her. We were all curious as hell, but it wasn't my business, so I kept my mouth shut. Eric Alan and JL came to find me one day. JL had a very serious look on her face.

"Cuz, what you know about Pa and that woman he hangs around with?"

I shrugged. "I don't know nothin'. I only see what you see."

"Hmph. Saddle up. We seen them together and are getting to the bottom of this little mystery."

Oh, well, I guess I was in, so off we went. Just like they said, we could see them down at the river. As soon as they spotted us, the woman mounted up and left, leaving Uncle Dockie alone. He got on his horse and waited for us. We rode to him and stopped. JL started in.

"All right, Pa, who is that woman?"

Uncle Dockie sat stone-faced. "None of your business, daughter."

"Hell to! Anything that goes on here concerning my ma is my business."

This was not well received by Uncle Dockie.

"Be damn careful, young'un. You're walking on thin ice here."

Now it was time for Eric Alan to get his big mouth involved. "Pa, I really don't blame you for havin' a little woman thing on the side, but don't you think it should stay in town?"

I realized I was right in the middle of a big family blowup. I had seen the same look on Uncle Dockie's face before and the result usually meant something was about to happen. He rode forward toward Eric Alan. I jumped my horse between them to block his path. When he had to stop, I grabbed his shirt.

"Uncle Dockie, your children are concerned and wanting answers. They're doing a damn poor job of asking, but when it comes to family, people get emotional."

Then JL said just the wrong thing. "Pa, if you are doing that woman, I'm going to tell Ma."

Now this really set him off. It was all I could do to keep them apart. So I started yelling, "Eric Alan and JL, you need to leave. I will stay here with Uncle Dockie. I said go, Goddammit!"

They turned and loped away. They had never shown any fear of their pa that I have ever witnessed, but this time I think I saw just a little bit of worry. At least enough concern to leave and avoid a fight. It was an emotional and stupid stunt, but they're family and we don't react as we might in another situation.

When they'd gone, I turned to Uncle Dockie. "Come sit with me for a while, please. We can talk this over."

He dismounted so I did also. We walked to a downed tree and sat. Nothing was said for what seemed like a long time. I wasn't going to say a word. I decided to wait him out.

He finally looked at me and said, "Thank you, Chris. Thank you for being here. Your level head is needed around here a lot. I hope you know that."

I did know that. My family connection is just separated enough that I can stay a little calmer. I rubbed his shoulder a little bit to get him calmed down.

"Uncle Dockie, you really need to tell them what is going on. They are very concerned. Their fear is that there is a problem between their ma and pa, the two people they love most in the world. This kind of thing is earth-shattering to young people."

"You're right, Chris. My behavior was no better than theirs. They are sitting on the top of that little hill, watching. Call them in."

I turned and waved my hat in the air. This brought them in and I must say with a little more respect. They got off their horses and we all stood and looked at each other. Uncle Dockie was the first to speak up.

"I'm sorry I lost my temper. I wasn't thinking like I should. That is the woman who found me on the Wet Beaver Creek and somehow got me home. She kept me on a horse while she walked for three days. I have no idea how she did it, but I owe my life to that little gal."

I thought JL would say 'awww,' but she didn't.

"Well, Pa, why in the Goddamn hell didn't you just say so? This sneaking around made us thinkin' awful thoughts. This really pisses me off."

Then Eric Alan had to vent a little. "You know, Pa, it's all right for me to do dumb stuff, but the thought of you out chasing nookie just ain't right."

I thought that might start another blowup, but just the opposite—it made them all laugh. JL walked over and gave her pa a big hug. She was very relieved. After a few seconds of this, she looked up into his eyes.

"Pa, why the big secret anyway?"

Uncle Dockie just shook his head. "She has some problems. Wants to stay hidden from the world. If that's what she wants, I will help her in any way I can."

JL said with a big frown, "That makes no sense at all, Pa. Haven't you asked her?"

"I know it sounds strange, but we have never said a word to each other. She just appears and gets close. I think she trusts me. Seems to be all she wants. Hell, I don't know."

Eric Alan was scratching his head. "Did it ever occur to you, Pa, to just ask?"

My Uncle Dockie can be the most sensitive person I have ever known. He responded, "I figure she will talk when she's ready. Can't push and help people feel safe at the same time. Got to just wait and let them come to it all by themselves."

This pretty much finished the whole mystery except for one last question from JL.

"Does Ma know about her, Pa?"

Uncle Dockie, with a look of confusion, said, "Well, of course, she does."

JL's face went cold. She punched her pa in the shoulder just like she does to me.

"All this time I have been worried about Ma, and she knew all along! Pa, you are a son of a bitch."

There was a big laugh from everyone. The fear was gone and everything was back to normal.

Chapter 36
The Mystery Unfolds

As the weeks went by, we continued to see the mysterious woman and Uncle Dockie together. They were seen in different places on the ranch. This mystery was driving JL crazy. She took every opportunity to spy on them. She hid on hilltops with a long glass and was dying to know what is going on. One day I saw her hiding behind a tree, so I took this as a great time to have some fun. I tied my horse some distance away and did the Apache sneak up, ending up right behind her.

"JL, what are you doing?"

She jumped so high I almost felt sorry for her. Remember, now, I said *almost*. When she figured out it was me, she calmed down and went back to spying through the long glass.

"Cuz, you are a big asshole and a sneaky son of a bitch..."

This was such a bonus for me. Hard to have more fun than this.

"JL, you should be ashamed of yourself. Spying on your ol' pa like this."

"Well, cuz, I should be, but I ain't. This is driving me crazy. Who is this woman? She is young, beautiful and hiding out here on the ranch. What the hell is going on?"

It was time to tell her what I knew. "I can tell you some about her," I admitted.

JL slowly turned and looked at me, her eyebrows raised. "Cuz , you son of a bitch, are you holding back on me?"

I stifled a chuckle. "I have to admit that I do know a little bit."

Her eyes got bigger and rounder. "Cuz, you better Goddamn well start talking if you want to live through this day."

Sometimes fun just goes on a roll, and I love every minute of it.

"I don't know, JL... I probably shouldn't say anything. It not being my business and all."

Now I had her going good. I started to walk away. She grabbed my sleeve and turned me around.

"I am serious! You start talking or things are about to get violent."

I guess I had milked it for all the fun I could get, so I started, "All right, JL, I will confide in you—but don't tell anyone or I look like a big loudmouth! On the way down to the gunfight in Naco, we ran into a bounty hunter your pa called Cim. He had this gal chained to a tree."

JL looked confused. "What gal?"

"The gal we are talking about. You know, the mystery woman with your pa. Bounty hunter said she had killed a man called Jasper Stone. Your pa paid him for her and let her go. She ran off like a deer. Right after that, you rode up."

She got quiet and you could see her thinking.

"Hmmm… Now I'm starting to understand. Pa saved her from the law and she saved him from the Apache raiding party. She is wanted and hiding out here on the ranch."

JL loved to punch my shoulder, but she really gave me a shot this time.

"Ow!" I protested.

"That's for not telling me, asshole. This has been tormenting me for days. Now I have something to tell you."

I stood there, waiting. "Well? Are you going to tell me?"

A big smile spread across her face. "No, don't think so."

Now, I know my cousin real well. She would tell me eventually because she wouldn't be able to stand not telling me. So I just didn't say any more.

A minute or two later, she turned from looking through the long glass and said, "They are talking. Pa must have waited her out. She and him are having quite the conversations now."

Now I was confused. "When are you going to tell me your secret?"

"I just did, dipshit. I swear you are as dumb as my brother. Her talking is a big event."

"All right, all right, if you say it's a big deal. It must be a woman thing. I got work to do, so I will leave you to your little drama."

As I left, she had that look on her face that I see quite often. You know, that expression women get when they think you're a dumbass. As I thought about it, I decided the woman talking was interesting. However, to ask Uncle Dockie about it would get me nowhere. I just went about my business and tried not to think about it too much. As I was riding away from my nosy cousin and rubbing my sore shoulder, I was thinking the fun was well worth the pain.

Chapter 37
The Old Stone Cabin

Remember back when I was learning to be a puncher and JL sent me to a little stone cabin located where the Verde River intersects with Hell Canyon? My job was to gather the cattle there and bring them back. Much to their surprise, I got it done, and boy was I proud of myself.

This little cabin was a place to spend the night when caught out too late in the day to get back to the ranch. This happens from time to time and no-one worries for a day or two. The ranch is big, and it takes a lot of time to get out to the work, get the work done and get back. This is exactly what happened to me.

I was gathering some cattle and it took most of the day, so I ran them into some corrals close to the little stone cabin. I like it there. It's quiet and cozy. Only thing you will hear is the sound of the river, a cow calling its calf, maybe a coyote, and for sure the breeze flowing through the trees. Don't tell anyone, but I have been known to stay an extra day and bask in the warm sun.

The cabin is a one-room affair. Has two sets of bunk beds. A table with chairs and a big handmade chair to sit by the fire. It has a huge stone fireplace and a cooking stove. A big roaring fire and a big plate of fried bacon are two of my favorite things in life.

When I walked in this time, things were different. The

C-Bar

place was clean. Blankets were on the bottom bunk. Someone was living here, and if I were to guess, it was a woman. I turned to close the door and was met with a pistol barrel in my face. It was too dark to know who it was, and I was in a sweat over this little surprise. When my eyes adjusted, I recognized the mysterious woman.

So this was her hideout! We just stared at each other for a few moments. I figured I had better start talking.

"I mean you no harm. I am Dockie's nephew, Chris Babb."

She was staring a hole through me, but finally responded, "I know who you are. I seen you when Dockie let me free from that bounty hunter. Dockie has told me all about you."

"I'm hoping it was good enough for you to lower that gun. Looking down a gun barrel makes me a mite nervous."

I think I saw a slight smile as she lowered her gun. "Dockie says you are someone he can trust. So I guess I will, too."

We both relaxed. All I could say was, "I got a slab of bacon. You hungry?"

She nodded her head and moved toward the stove. "I got biscuits baking. Bacon and biscuits will be a fine meal. I also robbed a bee hive."

We ate in silence. However, the meal was indeed good. A plate full of bacon and another plate piled high with biscuits smothered in butter and honey is just my kind of eating. I was not wanting to push conversation. She was slowly warming up to me. I have lived long enough to know that people either like me or hate me real quick. The people who dislike me are usually the ones who want to control those around them. They have a way of knowing who will let them and who won't. As they quickly figure me out and realize I don't fall in line with them being the leader, they resent me for it. Then comes the effort to get it done. When that intimidation doesn't work, they make it plain that I am not loved. On the other side, people who just want to get along in the world seem to take a liking to me. Somehow, they know I am not wanting to be in charge. They trust me not to take advantage of them. This mysterious woman was relaxing and trusting me.

Our conversation started with her asking about me.

"Chris, how is it you came to the C-Bar?"

Most people only want to talk about their own life. Don't really care about or are curious about others. The mysterious woman was not one of those. I told her my story. After I finished, she wanted to know about all the family members. I talked about each one. This was helping her to feel comfortable with everything going on around her.

After an hour of this, I looked at her and said, "I would like to know your name, but only if you are comfortable telling me."

She hesitated for a few moments before saying, "My name is Linda Kay Kern. I am hiding here because I am wanted for murder in Wickenburg."

"It's nice to meet you, Linda. That you are wanted means nothing to me. I get the feeling that there is more to the story. You don't seem like a killer. I'm thinking you were pushed into the problem. I'm going to tell you something, Linda, I'm not wrong very often about such things, and neither is Uncle Dockie. If he says you're good company, that's all I need to know."

Linda just stared at me. Seemed to be a shock to her. Then she relaxed and replied, "Thank you, Chris. Dockie told me all about his nephew. I hope you know the Barnett family loves you very much."

Her saying this caught me off guard a little bit. She got right to my core with that statement. I decided to give her a nudge.

"So, Linda, you know all about me and the Barnett family. I'm dying to know about you. How in the world did someone like you end up in this remote cabin, hiding from the law? This just doesn't add up for me."

"I can tell you my story of woe if you have some time and interest?"

"Well, it's dark outside. I have nowhere to go until tomorrow and I do have interest."

She stood up and started doing the dishes so I helped with the cleanup. After that, I built up the fire. She lay down on the bottom bunk and I climbed to the top bunk bed. After lying there for a few minutes, she started talking.

C-Bar

Chapter 38
Linda's Story

Here is how Linda told her story to me:

***

I was born on a farm just north of Fancy Prairie, Illinois. It was just my parents and me. I was an only child. We had a good life on that little farm. The ground could grow anything. Pa always said it was the best farm ground in the world. The dirt was rich and so flat water didn't know which way to run. There was lots of rain to keep it green and us prosperous.

I was a typical farm girl. Had livestock all around me. We all worked together. No schools of any kind, so Ma taught me readin' and writin'. I remember us all being happy. The seasons came and went, each having its good and bad points. Winters were cold and dreary. A lot of time was spent focusing on holidays and sitting by the fireplace. Pa was a good story teller. Staying warm and fed was always the priority. Pa used to say that firewood warmed you four times. Once when you cut it, twice when you split it, third time when you hauled it home and stacked it, and fourth when you burned it. It was a simple life for sure.

I was fifteen when Ma passed away. She just wasted away and died. I was told by the doctor that she had the cancer. This was real hard on Pa and me. When a close-knit family has a loss like this, it takes the joy out of everything. Pa and I just hunkered down and worked harder. The work seemed to help us cope with our loss. A year later, Pa was cutting firewood and fell over dead. Doctor said his heart just gave out. Then it was only me. A sixteen-year-old girl can't make a farm work, so I needed to make some changes. There was a family close by that came to see me. I met them at the door.

"Hi, Linda, I think you know us. I'm Robert Martin; this is my wife Mary. The little one here is Bessie. Can we come in and talk?"

I brought them in and we all sat at the table.

Mr. Martin had this to say: "We have bought a forty-acre piece of ground in Greensboro, Kansas. We have a wagon and a team of oxen to pull it. We know you are leaving and have no real place to go, so if you want, you are welcome to go with us. The trip will be hard but it's an opportunity to get a new start."

It took me no time at all to decide to go with them. Since I had no options, I was greatly relieved. They were a nice family. We left a week later. Mr. Martin was correct when he said it was a hard trip. The going was slow with the oxen pulling the wagon. Mary and Bessie rode most of the way while Mr. Martin and I walked. We just kept trudging along day after day. The roads were rough to travel on, and the rivers were even harder to get across. We camped every night on the trail. Sometimes we met people coming and going, and sometimes we saw no-one for days at a time. Mr. Martin was always close to his rifle.

He told us at the campfire one evening, "Desperate times will make anyone do things they would not normally do. Watching your family starve will make a man kill if he has to. If anyone ever tells you that they would never hurt others to survive, he has never been desperate. We need to be careful at all times. We are surrounded by desperate people."

Truer words were never spoken. Many times we met people on the trail, giving up on their dreams and going back East. Broken men with starving families. We heard their stories and shared what we could with them. Mr. Martin never gave in to the fear of failing. We just kept going.

After dark one evening, we heard our horses being upset with something. We got up to look and could see a man leading one of our oxen away. Mr. Martin shot, and we all could see the man fall. The oxen came walking back. The next morning, we left and didn't go see if the man was dead or not. We just wanted to move on.

When we got to Kansas, it was easy to tell the country was very different. The earth was not good for growing crops. This was very disappointing to us all. Our moods were not as good as earlier. We finally arrived in Greensboro. Worn out and not feeling good about our great adventure. We all went into the local land office.

C-Bar

Mr. Martin said, "Hello, sir. We own some land nearby and were hoping you could show us to it."

The man behind the desk responded, "Let me see your paperwork." He looked it over and then said, "You own a parcel just north of town. Let me get out the map."

He spread out a map on the table. We all gathered around to see where it was. Truthfully, it didn't mean too much to us.

"Let me take you folks out to your land, and we can walk your boundary lines."

We left and were very nervous as to what we would find. Outside of town a mile or so was our parcel. Flat, barren and very disappointing. All we could do at that point was make camp and try to figure out our next move. Over the next few months, we built a small house and were living poor. Mr. Martin ended up in town working as a school teacher. I was getting any work I could find to help keep us alive. Our great dream had busted.

Maybe I was desperate or just young, but I thought I fell in love with a cowboy who came through. He was loud, bold, good looking and talking big stories about getting rich in Wickenburg, Arizona Territory. We found each other on Main Street. He was all over me trying to get my attention and it worked. Said his name was Jasper Stone. Next thing I know, he proposes to me and wants me to go with him to Arizona. Truth is I had nothing in Kansas, so I told the Martins goodbye and off we went.

We rode for several days. The land was getting even more barren. When we arrived in Wickenburg, I was not impressed. Small, dusty little town and hot. He found us a little cabin and we set up house. That is when things started going wrong.

Jasper would disappear for days at a time. Sometimes a week or two. Then he would walk in with his usual behavior as if he had not done anything wrong. He would demand that I sleep with him and then he would go downtown and get drunk for a few days. Every night he would come home drunk and angry.

He'd yell, "Woman, get your clothes off! We have business to attend to."

I had nothing to do with that. "That ain't going to happen. I don't want no whore house diseases."

This would set him off into a rage. He would beat on me for a while and then usually pass out and sleep on the floor with the scorpions crawling on him. Next day he would crawl out the door make his way downtown and do it all over again. The beatings got worse and worse. Then he would disappear again. This was always a relief for me. The neighbor ladies were quick in telling me that he had built a reputation as a man willing to do anything for money. I'm sure he was stealing cattle and making his money that way. This was my life for about six months.

After a long absence, he broke down the front door late one night and was even drunker than usual. All he had to do was turn the door knob, but he shattered the door instead. With a rage, he came at me. His eyes were wide and evil looking.

He was screaming, "You bitch, you're going to do things my way or die tonight!"

Jasper had a problem. He left a gun in the house just in case I ever needed to protect myself. I was ready for him. I had the pistol in my hand. As he outstretched his arms to grab me, I shot him in the chest. After the smoke cleared and I realized he was dead, all I could do was sit there and try and figure out what to do.

The neighbors must have gone to the sheriff because he showed up and asked, "What happened here?"

I told the truth—"He came at me one too many times and I killed him."

The sheriff looked everything over and then had his help carry off the body. He told me not to leave until all this was figured out. The next day he came back. "Linda Kern," he said, "you are under arrest for the murder of Jasper Stone."

I was already in shock, but this was something I had not even thought about. He put iron cuffs on me and took me to jail. So there I was in a hell hole, waiting for something to happen.

Two days later a man in a suit walks in with the sheriff. "Mrs. Kern," the sheriff said, "this is your lawyer. He has been appointed by the judge to represent you."

I felt some relief for a short while. Turns out my lawyer was a drunk and worthless. Every time he came to see me, I had to tell him everything all over again. He kept forgetting my story. Two weeks of that and my trial day came.

Judge brought the trial to order and said, "The prosecution needs to tell us what went on here."

A man in a suit but sober-looking stood up. "Your Honor, we are here because one Linda Kay Kern willfully and for no reason killed in cold blood one Jasper Stone with a pistol. We are here to prove beyond a reasonable doubt that she is guilty of murder."

This struck fear in my heart.

Judge spoke again. "The defense will enter a plea."

What happened then was beyond belief.

"Your Honor, the defense is entering a plea of guilty as charged and a plea for mercy."

I about passed out. Words were not coming out of my mouth. It was all I could do to stand up.

The judge just looked at me and then said, "Linda Kay Kern, I sentence you to twenty years at Yuma prison. Court dismissed."

I don't even remember being taken back to jail. Overnight, I had come to realize that my life was over. I have been down some hard roads, but this was the worst time of my life. The night before I was to leave for Yuma, the sheriff came to my cell.

He said, "You are leaving for Yuma tomorrow. However, I have a deal for you. Get naked with me and I will let you slip out of here tonight."

When someone tells me things they would never do I just have to laugh at them. He came in, and I did what he wanted. It was a sickening experience, but I got through it. The man was drunk, dirty and smelled terrible. It's almost funny now, but afterwards he fell asleep. I knew he was lying about letting me go but I knew that was my chance. I slipped out of the bunk, got dressed and was leaving when I turned around and picked up his clothes. It was easy to then lock him in the cell. The next day, him trying to explain this had to be rather funny.

I went into the front office to find no-one there. Stuffing his clothes in the stove and watching them burn was a wonderful thing to see. There was some money in the desk and a pistol hanging on a hook. They were coming with me. There was a small barn out back that kept the horses. I slipped in there, picked a horse, saddled him up and away I went. The direction I went was just an accident. It ended up being north.

Yarnell

Going north meant going uphill—and I mean *uphill*. It was hard going. A narrow path was all there was. The sun was coming up, and I knew I could be seen for miles, so it was time to hide under a rock and get through the day. My big problem was no food or water. This country is unforgiving to people in my position. I suffered through the long hot day and was worse for the wear. At dark I went on up the hill. At the top I was played out. There were a few lights up ahead, and I had no options, so that was my destination. This little place was called Yarnell from the sign on the road. The first house I came to was where I went. I knocked on the door that was opened by an older man.

I said, "Excuse me, sir. I am thirsty, hungry and in general in very poor condition. Can you help me?"

He turned to someone inside and said, "Irene, come help me. I got a little gal in trouble here."

The man was helping me inside when his wife came into the room.

"Lordy. Lordy, young lady! You are a mess."

I could barely get the words out. "Yes, ma'am, I surely am."

"Harry help me get her inside," the lady said.

They laid me on a couch and started pouring water down my throat. When I rested for a while, the food started coming. I truly believe these people saved my life. They never asked me why I was in this condition, only nursed me back to health. I think they suspected my plight but never probed with questions. Harry cared for my horse and Irene mothered me. These were damn fine people. Two days later, I was ready to leave.

With tears in my eyes I told them, "I would have perished were it not for your help. I will always appreciate your helping me like you have. I really need to go because I don't want to bring trouble for you."

They understood. Never asked me what was the trouble. Just loved on me for a while and wished me luck. Harry brought my horse around and he looked much better. There were saddle bags filled with food and a big canteen with water strapped to the horn. I tear up just thinking about these people. There are a lot of horrible people in the world, but I truly believe there are more good folks than bad.

Prescott

Three days of night travel and I was looking at Prescott. I was tired again and wore out, but I had a plan. Asking around, I was pointed toward the local stable. Inside was an older gentleman.

He said, "What can I do for you, young lady?"

"Thought you might buy my horse and saddle?" I said.

He looked my borrowed horse over real careful. Then he examined the saddle. When he turned to me, I was hoping he wouldn't know it was stolen.

"I would go fifty dollars and ask no questions."

I put out my hand. "Deal?"

He paid me, and it was time to look for a room somewhere. He seemed like a good ol' boy, so I started with him.

"I'm looking for a cheap room. Got any ideas?"

"If you are good with horses, I need help, and a room in back is part of the deal."

I responded, "Well, I have been scooping horse manure my whole life. The only kind of work I know is hard work. I would love and need the job."

"My name is Howard. I own this place," he said. Ol'

Howard was scratching his chin and thinking. "I feel good about you, young lady. What be your name?"

That question caught me off guard, but I recovered. "Nancy, sir," I said. "Nancy Smith."

He chuckled and I don't think he believed me, but it didn't seem to matter to him.

"Well, Nancy, the room is in back. Go on in and rest. I do believe you need some sleep. You can start tomorrow morning."

I needed some things first, so off I went to Whiskey Row. First thing I did was gather up some work clothes. Then it was to a Chinese bath house. My God, how that felt to sink into hot water! Afterwards, I started looking for a cafe to get some food. I walked along the street and was noticing that no-one was paying any attention to me. That was a big relief. I entered a cafe and sat down. A big woman walked up to get my order.

"Hello, hun," she said. "I'm called Norma. What can I get you?"

I ordered meat loaf, mashed potatoes, green beans and coffee.

Off she went, and I could swear the floor was shaking with every step she took. She came back soon with the plate of food and it was without a doubt wonderful. The kind of wonderful that made my stomach tingle with every bite. After eating I went to the stable and found my room. Got comfortable and fell asleep. Twelve hours later, it was five a.m and I was up and waiting for Howard.

He walked in at five thirty and said, "Nancy, we don't start around here until seven. If I were you I would get something to eat. You have time."

He didn't have to tell me twice. I found Norma again and chowed down. Things were looking up.

Cim

Life really wasn't too bad. For the next month, I worked and felt stronger every day. Howard was a good man to work for and Norma was becoming a good friend. Other than those two people, I kept low and stayed to myself. Didn't need any attention coming my way.

One morning I was up before dark and walked into the barn. I was grabbed up and walked off with! I fought to get away at first but soon figured that fighting was useless. Whoever had me was strong enough to have his way. In the back alley, he put handcuffs on me and threw me on a horse. Off we went. An hour later, we rode up to a camp out in the middle of nowhere. He pulled me off the horse and chained me to a tree. When the sun came up, I was looking things over and found two more people chained to trees also. I figured the man who grabbed me was probably a bounty hunter and the men also his prisoners.

He said, "My name is Cim. I am a bounty hunter. These other two fine looking men are John Doe and Pecos Bill. They are dangerous men and crazy to boot. Now, I'm going to get some rest, and if I get woke up I'll beat hell out of whoever is the problem. Savvy?"

I just nodded my head. About an hour later, up walked you, Dockie and a man called Bobby. Dockie and Bobby knew the bounty hunter from the past. They visited for a bit when Dockie asked about me. You know that part of the story.

Dockie had put some money in my pocket and off I went. I asked him later why he did that.

He explained, "I had some dealings with Jasper Stone. He's the kind of man that would try and seduce his best friend's wife. When I found out you killed him, I liked you immediately."

After he let me go, I was off and running again. I managed to get back to the stable. Howard was waiting for me, so I gave him a brief explanation, hoping he wouldn't keep me for the law.

"Well, young lady, I've gotten to know you over the last month. You ain't a bad one. Let's get you fixed up to ride. Might as well give you back your stolen horse. I also have an old mule that is good for nothing except packing. He's yours also."

I gathered up my gear and was leaving when Howard handed me twenty dollars. He said, "It's back pay I owe you." I don't reckon it was. But then he said, "Good luck, young lady. Hope to see you again under more pleasant circumstances. Now go slow out of town and don't draw attention."

With tears in my eyes, I said, "Thanks, Howard. You're a good man."

On the way out of town I bought as much food as I could load on my mule. There was also a lot of things I needed for the trail. When all my money was gone, I did just what Howard told me to do. I rode out quiet and then went into a long trot heading east.

Wet Beaver Creek

So, I traveled east for several days. My plan was to get as far away as possible—someplace where they would not know I was wanted. Back to Illinois didn't sound bad. Someplace, anyplace just far, far away. Suddenly, before me was the most beautiful place I had ever seen. A canyon with tall red cliffs. There were huge cottonwood trees lining a river. The river was not deep or very wide, but the water was crystal clear. It felt remote and safe. I was travel weary and needed to rest. This seemed like a place to stay for a while. There were places to explore before deciding on a camp site when I smelled smoke. This was alarming, but I figured it could be a good thing. Anyone here would never know about my trouble, so exploring it seemed to make sense. Up river about a quarter-mile was a small stone cabin. Smoke was coming out the chimney.

I called out, "Hello in the house. Anyone home?"

It didn't take long for a man to come out carrying a rifle. He was older and skinny. Looked poorly.

"I'm here. What you want?" he barked.

"Just traveling east and smelled your smoke. I mean you no harm."

The old man looked me over for a few seconds. Seemed to soften up a bit. He said, "What's a young gal doing out here in the wilderness. You lost?"

"No, sir, not lost. Just tired, wore down and hungry."

"Put your horse in that corral, young lady. There is graze and water for him there. He don't look any better than you do. Then come on in and eat something."

He turned and went back inside. I wasn't feeling afraid of him, but my pistol was tucked away just in case. Entering the cabin was a surprise. It was clean and tidy. Biscuits and gravy were on a stove.

The man pointed toward a chair. "Sit down, sweetheart. You're just in time to eat, and from the looks of you, a meal will do you some good."

I relaxed. This man had put me at ease. His voice and mannerisms told me he was a kind person. He filled a plate and handed it to me. I went after it and didn't look up until it was gone.

He was watching me eat. Then he said with a soft and kind voice, "Young lady, what is so wrong in your world that you arrive here in the condition you are in?"

All I could say was, "Got time for a story?"

He just nodded his head. So I told him my story, same as I'm telling you. Afterward, he just pondered.

Then he said, "World can't find you here, baby girl. Stay as long as you need to."

I can get emotional when I'm wore down to a nub. I started crying and couldn't stop. He came over to me and pulled me to his chest while I cried. After a spell, he walked me over to his bunk. I lay down and went to sleep. The first good sleep in a very long time.

When I woke up, he was gone. I panicked for a minute, thinking he went after the law, so I went outside looking around. I found him down by the river sitting in a handmade chair. He looked up at me and motioned for me to sit in a grassy spot next to him, so I did. We sat not talking for a few minutes.

Then he finally said, "Well, you told me your story, so I will tell you mine. I'm old and dying. This is the most beautiful place in the world, so I came here to finish my life. To sit by this river and bask in the warm sun is a little piece of heaven. The Lord and I are talking, and he will take me when the time is right."

It was my turn to love on him, so I did just that. He seemed to appreciate it a great deal.

He looked at me and said, "Looks like two wounded birds found each other. I'm old and leaving this world, and you are young and trying to stay in it. Ain't life a mystery?"

All I could do was nod my head. Then he told me his name was Kenneth Johnson.

Life with Kenneth

Life was good for the next two months. Kenneth needed me and I needed him. We became close and confided in each other. He had his story in this world and I had mine. Sometimes I ponder on that facts of life. Everyone alive has their own story and every one is different.

We were sitting next to the river holding hands when Kenneth passed away. I felt like an orphan again, alone and scared to death about tomorrow. It felt like everyone I ever loved in this world wasn't around long. My mind tells me it's not my fault, but my heart wonders if it's something about me that makes this happen...

I buried Kenneth in a sandy area next to the river. As I sat there making a grave marker and grieving, there was the sound of gunfire up river. I wondered if I should I run or see who it was. My curiosity was stronger than my fear, so upriver I went.

It wasn't long before a body was floating down river. It came close to me, so I reached out to pull it ashore. To my surprise it was the man who'd set me free from the bounty hunter and he was still alive. It was your Uncle Dockie! You already know what happened to him with them Apaches. Getting him out of the river was not easy, but I got it done.

When it seemed safe I carried and dragged this man back to the cabin. Once I had him inside, the task at hand was to dress his wounds and stop the bleeding. It was nip and tuck on him living, but of course you know he did. Three days later, he was able to talk enough to tell me how to get him home. There was only one horse, so he rode and I walked. After three days and forty tough miles, we arrived late in the evening. I knocked on the door and was met by a woman with a shotgun in my face.

"I mean no harm to anyone. I have your husband out here and he is hurt bad," I told her.

From there, we got him into the house and in bed. When the woman finished checking him out head to foot, she asked me what happened.

I explained everything to her, including my dire position. She thought this over for a few moments then responded, "Thank you for saving my dear husband's life. I know what he would tell me to do. You can't stay here, so I will pack you plenty of food. You go upstream until the river meets Hell Canyon. There is a stone cabin there. You will be safe. Wait for Dockie to come."

So, that's what I did. Finding the cabin was easy. I've been here for several days, and then you walked in the door.

***

That is the story as she told me. The sun was up by the time she finished, and I needed to get the cattle back to the ranch. On the way back, my mind was working hard. There was only one way for this to go, and by God, I was going to make it happen.

Chapter 39
Back to the Stone Cabin

Four days later, Uncle Dockie and I rode up to the cabin. She must have seen us coming and walked out to meet us. Linda was a lonely woman and glad to see us.

After some hugging, Uncle Dockie said, "Linda, we have a plan. Let's go in and talk about this problem."

She seemed surprised that there was a plan. Inside and sitting at the table, it was my turn to talk.

"Linda, I came here from Chicago as I told you. What I didn't tell you is that I was a lawyer back there. I understand how to work with politicians. We are going to get you a pardon or die trying. You also can't stay out here all alone. You need to come to the ranch with us."

A look of concern crossed her face. "Someone will see me and the law will come. That is a bad idea for you and the ranch."

Uncle Dockie said, "We got that all figured out. Tell her, Chris."

"You are my sister from Chicago. You will stay in my cabin with Sara and me. I live just enough out of the way that if the law ever came snooping around, you could slip away. You really don't have much to say about this. Aunt Marsha sent us for you."

With that said, we gathered up Linda's few possessions and went home. I introduced her to everyone at the ranch as my sister, Nancy. She was here for a few months visiting. Everyone was glad to have her on the ranch, especially the young punchers. I was amazed at how she looked after Aunt Marsha and JL got done with her. Damn fine looking woman.

Chapter 40
The Plan

If there is one thing I know, it's politicians. Uncle Dockie and I feel the same about them. It's all about votes and it takes money to get votes. The territorial governor was in Phoenix, so a trip was planned. I decided to go alone. My suitcase was packed with my lawyer clothes. I had a briefcase full of papers to rummage through when I needed to pretend to be an attorney. I took a stage down and headed for the den of thieves.

When I got there, people were waiting outside the governor's office. The man at the desk told me I had to wait my turn and that could mean several days. I just got in his face.

"My name is Christian Babb. I'm an attorney wanting to make a campaign contribution."

Now I had his attention.

"Mr. Babb, how much contribution are you wanting to make?"

"I have twenty-five hundred dollars in my briefcase."

"Just a minute, Mr. Babb. I will see if the governor is available." He disappeared and returned shortly with the expected, "The governor will see you now."

I was introduced to the governor who jumped up and was the most congenial man in the world. This is a quality that any successful politician must have. The ability to feign caring is their first stock in trade.

"Sit down, Mr. Babb," he said graciously. "Tell me how I can help you."

"I'm here, Governor, for two reasons," I began.

I reached into my briefcase and pulled out a fat envelope full of money. I put it on his desk, but on my edge and not where he could reach it.

"The first reason is to make a campaign contribution of twenty-five hundred dollars."

He looked at the envelope and then started figuring me out. "And just what is the second reason?"

"I'm here representing Linda Kay Kern. She was unjustly convicted of killing her husband. The Wickenburg defense lawyer is a drunk and did a horrible job for her. She should have been let go for the reason of self-defense. Any sober lawyer could have had the matter set aside in the investigation phase. We are requesting a pardon for her, sir."

The governor thought over the matter for a while, then asked, "So, is this woman in prison?"

"No, sir, she is at large."

He was starting to figure out the proposition I was making. "And just how and why is she at large?"

"She escaped, Governor."

The governor then yelled for his assistant to come in. "Escort Mr. Babb out of the building, please."

This surprised me. I know it's not possible for a successful politician to be honest. I was scratching my head over this, for sure. I stood up, gathered up the money and said one more thing.

"If for some reason there is a change of heart, you can find me in Prescott. Good day, sir."

I was a very disappointed pretend lawyer at this moment in time. All I could do was go home.

C-Bar

Chapter 41
Behan

I had been home for a week. The family was inside the main house eating, when Sheriff Johnny Behan and three deputies rode up. Uncle Dockie and I went out to see what he wanted.

"Dockie, I'm here because I have gotten word that you are harboring a fugitive named Linda Kay Kern. I'm here to take her in."

Uncle Dockie didn't have time to respond because Aunt Marsha came out of the house with her shotgun in hand. She walked off the porch and right up to Behan. She put the barrel in his stomach. "Behan, there is no-one here you want. If you don't leave, I will blow you right out of that saddle."

Behan looked up at Uncle Dockie. Uncle Dockie was leaning against a porch support pole, rolling a cigarette. He just looked up and smiled. "You look to be in a bad spot, Behan. Were I you, I might just mosey down the road. When Marsha acts like this, I make dust."

Behan then looked down at Aunt Marsha. He saw the crazy look in her eyes and didn't say a word. He turned his horse and rode away. Aunt Marsha turned and walked back inside. Uncle Dockie and I were amused by this, but I had to speak on the matter.

"Uncle Dockie, he will be back. Next time he will have more people behind him. No way he can let this humiliation go without another try."

Uncle Dockie nodded because he knew this to be true. We walked back inside, and I spoke to the family.

"We need to be ready for him to come back again. He will return with more help. When anyone sees them coming, fire a shot. Linda, you can just fade away. If you're not in my cabin, get there quick. We will make a way for you to not be found. They will eventually give up."

A week later, Behan returned with twelve soldiers. A shot was fired, and we were ready.

He rode up to the front of the house and called out, "Dockie, I have all the help I need to make this happen. If you resist, we will be forced to search this ranch by force."

We were all on the porch when Aunt Marsha came out. "Well, hello, Johnny. Glad to see you. Your men are more than welcome to get down and rest in the shade."

This was not what Behan was expecting. He started looking around like an ambush was planned. He turned to the men behind him, ordering, "Scatter out and find this woman. She is here somewhere and be damn careful! These people ain't usually this nice."

They all dismounted and looked in every building. The soldiers looked high and low. Fifteen minutes later, the sergeant walked up to Behan, saying, "She ain't here, sir."

Behan was not happy with this. He knew we had hidden her. He turned to us with cold eyes.

"You think you are too smart for us," he growled. "Here is the next order of business. A two thousand dollar bounty will be put up for Linda Kay Kern. The people coming next won't be bound by the same restrictions I am. Bring her out now before things get ugly."

Behan got no response from Uncle Dockie but Aunt Marsha had something to say.

"Well, Johnny, your rude behavior is very disappointing. You're usually such a polite young man."

It became a stare down contest. His face turned a dark red. He turned and rode away. A few minutes later, Linda came out from hiding. We returned to the house and the mood was very somber.

Linda said quietly, "It's time I left before someone gets hurt."

She was covered up with objection to this statement. So much in fact she didn't argue. A few minutes later, Tucson came in the door.

"What in the hell is going on out here? Half the Union army just left the place."

I took Tucson outside and gave him the story. He really didn't respond very much. He just got on his horse and left. This was unlike him, but hell, I never know what he is thinking.

The days passed with no problems. Linda was well entrenched in our family. Liz loved her dearly. Liz, Linda, and I lived together. We all got along well. I couldn't decide if the girls were more mother and daughter, or sisters. Liz needed this woman in her life. I tried, but I'm just not as good at knowing what is going on with a little girl as Linda. They connected on a level I couldn't seem to find. I wasn't upset with that; I was just glad Liz had a woman to be close to.

Chapter 42
Big Mike

Mike is someone you don't want mad at you and threatening anyone in the C-Bar family is not a good idea. He told Uncle Dockie he was going to be gone for a few days and off he went. Mike made his grand entrance in several Prescott saloons.

"I'm here to make an announcement. Anyone that tells a bounty hunter where the C-Bar is will answer to me. If a bounty hunter finds his way to the C-Bar, I will let him live long enough to tell where he got his information. God help you if I find out just who it might be."

Wasn't long before he was arrested. Behan said he was obstructing justice.

Mike responded, "You're Goddamn right, I am. You can throw me in jail if you want, but remember something—I have a long memory."

All that statement got him was a quick trip to the jail house. He didn't go easy and this made things even worse. A few days later, we were wondering about Mike when we got word he was in jail in Prescott. This riled us up some so JL, Eric Alan Uncle Dockie and I went to see about his trouble.

When we walked into the jail we were met by Behan, who said cockily, "Your man is in jail for obstructing justice and resisting arrest. If you are here to bail him out, just do so; but if you're here for trouble, remember one thing—you are not in your stronghold. You are in my town."

I said nonchalantly, "No trouble from us. How much is bail?"

"Two hundred and fifty."

We pooled our money and came up with that amount. Mike was let out.

When we met up, he said, "Sorry for your trouble. This asshole took me away from my work, so I think I'll get back to it."

Uncle Dockie looked confused. "What work is that, Mike?"

"I'm here to make sure bounty hunters get a big warning about coming to the C-Bar."

Now we all understood. Uncle Dockie rubbed him arm and said,
"Mike, we need you at the ranch. If trouble comes, you can't help if you are in town."

Mike seemed to understand and we all walked out. As we left town, Mike rode his horse into the Palace and made one more announcement.

"You all know and had better take heed. Any bounty hunter comes to the C-Bar, I'm coming back to town, and it will be hell to pay."

The Palace's owner was mad but knew better than to say anything. For emphasis, Mike's horse took a dump in the saloon on his way out. Pretty funny really.

C-Bar

Chapter 43
Trouble While We Were Gone

On our way back to the ranch, we had a strange meeting. Coming down the road toward us was a huckster wagon. There were, from time to time, people who operated a traveling small store out of a wagon that came to the ranch looking to do a little trading. These wagons were always carrying household items like pots and pans. They would buy, sell and trade for anything that could be carried in their wagon. The newest labor saving device was always the new and best items ever invented. We always treated them with courtesy because they were trying to make an honest living and we appreciated that. This one, however, was a bit different. The huckster was tied up in his wagon and the horses were merrily going down the road. We stopped the team and untied the man.

Dockie asked, "Mister, were you robbed and tied up?"

Here is what he said: "Hell, no. I went to that C-Bar Ranch and got treated with complete disrespect. I didn't get a chance to even open my mouth before I was attacked, bound and thrown in my wagon. I hope they all die of the plague."

This was suspicious because we knew that didn't happen. An idea came to me.

"You say the C-Bar Ranch is that way?" I pointed in

the direction he had traveled from. "We are bounty men, looking for the place."

He looked at me while wiping the sweat from his face. "We share that occupation, boys. This wagon is how I get close enough to get people off guard. That outfit is on the ready. I don't think you will have much success. Place is like an armed army camp."

We all burst out laughing. Big Mike was on him real quick.

Mike looked at us and said, "Well, what do you think would be a good thing for our bounty hunter? I want to send a good warning to the townsfolk."

We discussed this for a while when we came up with a plan. We stripped the man down to his shorts. Mike lifted him on one of the horses, facing backward. He was tied on the horse with his hands tied behind him. I found some paint and wrote on the wagon: BOUNTY HUNTERS BEWARE. We hit his horses in the butt and they were off to Prescott. Later on, we heard rumors about him coming into town with the townspeople enjoying his entertaining entrance down Whiskey Row.

When we returned to the ranch, we heard the story. Aunt Marsha enjoyed filling us in. Aunt Marsha and Winston were sitting on the porch when the man had rolled up to the house. He came in like they all do, selling the newest and biggest household items that we just couldn't live without. Problem was he kept looking around as if he was searching for something. That was his mistake. Every salesman knows to focus on the woman of the house. They are the decision makers for his wares. He was even trying to sell Winston some pots and pans.

Aunt Marsha commented, "He just didn't fit the mold. His stay didn't last long until he decided to head back to Prescott. We may have helped him make that decision."

C-Bar

Chapter 44
The Governor's Summons

A shot was fired. Linda went to her hiding spot. I walked down to the house. Behan was there looking for me.

"Chris Babb," he said very officially, "I have a summons from the governor. You are to go to his office."

This sounded bad. Really bad. I was sure the governor tipped off Behan about Linda being here. He didn't even give my bribe a second's thought. I was thinking he would file bribery charges against me. If that were the case, I was in as much trouble as Linda. We went inside to read the summons.

I studied it for a while when Aunt Marsha asked, "What does he want you for, Chris?"

I shook my head. "I really don't know, Aunt Marsha. It just says to come see him. I will go and find out, I guess."

As I left, Uncle Dockie followed me out. "I don't like this, Chris. I'm going with you. You may very well need help."

I didn't object. I was real concerned and needed company. We left the next day. People were concerned that I may not return. Linda was beside herself with worry. It felt like a long trip getting there. When we walked into the governor's office, his assistant was up immediately, ushering us in. I was completely confused! This didn't feel like I was about to be arrested.

The governor welcomed us in. Uncle Dockie was stone faced and that can be real scary.

The governor began, "Thank you for coming to my office. I will get to the point. You have friends in high places. Wells Fargo did a complete investigation on this matter, and you were correct about how Linda Kay Kern was treated. According to their extensive investigation, Miss Kern was indeed the victim here and not the criminal. I might add that this investigation must have cost Wells Fargo a huge amount of money. You are well connected in this world."

He handed us a piece of paper. I looked at it. Uncle Dockie could only kind of read, so I thought it best to explain it to him.

"Uncle Dockie, this is a pardon for Linda signed by the governor."

We both looked back at the man. We were without words. Finally, Uncle Dockie asked, "Governor, does this mean that Linda and Chris are off the hook?"

"Yes, it does. The pardon is for all past and present crimes. As for Chris, here, I have decided he was just doing what he could for his client." He then looked at us with a big smile. We all had to laugh over this.

I said, "So, Governor, does this mean that I have finally found my first honest politician?"

He chuckled. "Well, Mr. Babb, you may have found your first half-honest politician. Wells Fargo is a big supporter of mine."

We all laughed again.

"Governor," Uncle Dockie stated, "I will take a half-honest man every time. Chris and I have to go. We have some very anxious people at home waiting for some answers."

The governor put his hand out to shake, and we obliged him. He added, "Just remember, you have a friend in me. Any problems, just let me know."

C-Bar

Chapter 45
Tucson Wins the Day

On the way home from meeting with the governor, we picked up Tucson in Prescott. He was coming back to the ranch whether he wanted to or not. We found him in his office. Uncle Dockie started in on him.

"Tucson, you crafty old son of a bitch! We have in this briefcase a pardon for Linda. How did you make that happen?"

All smiles, Tucson told his story. "I have been the enforcer for Wells Fargo for the last ten years. They love my ass. I have the job I have now because they appreciate what I did for them over the years. Old man Fargo told me they owed me a favor, and when that time came to just ask. I got on a train and found him pronto. I walked into his office and started to tell him the story when he interrupted me.

"He said, 'I really don't care what the story is, Tucson. Anything you say I will swear to.' He handed me a paper of Wells Fargo stationery. The top page had his signature at the bottom and an official Wells Fargo seal on it.

"He said, 'Just write up what you want and finish on the page I signed. After that, it's all yours to do what you want.' Can you beat that?

"All the way back to Prescott, though, I was trying to

figure out what I was going to say. Trouble is my writing ain't very good. I have an educated assistant who's damn good at all this and even has a writing machine. I told him the story and he composed the entire letter. It was so damn good, I didn't understand one word. We worked on it day and night until it sounded like something a dumbass like me didn't write. With that done, I went to Phoenix and barged into the governor's office like someone important. He looked it over, bought the story and sent for you. Am I a smart son of a bitch or what?" The grin across his face couldn't have been bigger.

Uncle Dockie grabbed Tucson and kissed him on the side of his head.

"Tucson, let's go home. Get your little girl and let's go. I got a buggy waiting."

On the way out the door, Uncle Dockie asked, "So how many detectives did you have doing this investigation, anyway?"

"Wells Fargo had twelve detectives and three lawyers working on this little matter."

I asked next, "But why would the governor think Wells Fargo cared enough to spend that kind of money?"

Tucson smiled real big. "Ah, well… you see, that might be because he thinks Linda Kay Kern is Fargo's niece."

We laughed about that for an hour.

C-Bar

Chapter 46
Home

We got home a few hours later. When we walked up on the porch, we could hear a big fight going on in the house. Eric Alan was sitting on the porch swing, swinging like he didn't have a care in the world.

Uncle Dockie gave him a questioning look.

"Don't go in there, Pa. The women are fighting, and I ain't brave enough to try and stop them. Hell, just listen to them go on."

So we did. I could hear Aunt Marsha loud and clear. She was talking loudly and then stamped her foot.

"Young lady, you ain't going nowhere!"

I had never seen Aunt Marsha so mad that she stomped her foot. This was a new one on me.

Then it was JL's turn. "Really, Linda, Ma has the final word around here, and she says you are staying. Might as well give up your try."

Then Linda yelled, "I'm going, and that is all there is to say about it! Me staying is just going to bring on trouble and get someone hurt. *I ain't worth it!*"

Then we heard a slap. I looked at Eric Alan and Uncle Dockie, somewhat shocked. I said quietly, "Is that what

C-Bar

I think it was?" All they could do was nod, wide-eyed. "Well, boys, all I can say is that I have been on the receiving end of getting slapped by Aunt Marsha. Linda has no idea what she is getting herself into."

Eric Alan added, "Amen to that. You and me both, cuz."

We got brave enough to look through the window. Things turned physical. Aunt Marsha and JL were on each side of Linda and were dragging her to the couch. They sat her down and were on both sides, holding her down. The yelling just got louder.

Uncle Dockie looked at us and said, "Men, it's time we went in there and each grabbed a woman. They are going to hurt each other."

"Hell to, Pa! Sis would make quick work out of me. I've been scared of her my whole life. She's mean as a badger when she gets riled. I ain't going in there."

I stepped up with, "It's up to me, boys. Wish me luck."

Uncle Dockie gave me a look of mock sadness. "Good luck, nephew. Been nice knowing you."

In I went. They were on the couch grappling with each other. I walked in front of them and (from a distance, I might add) held up the pardon. Aunt Marsha scowled at me.

"Chris, we don't have time for you. Now, get!"

I stood my ground, holding up the pardon. Eventually, it got JL's attention.

"Wait a minute, Ma. We need to read what Chris has."

They stopped fighting and all read the pardon. It took a minute to sink in. Then, in an instant, they went from fighting to loving on each other and crying. Eventually, Aunt Marsha asked me how I got it done.

I held up both my hands. "I didn't do it. Tucson was the one who made this happen."

"Tucson? Well, where is he?"

They looked around and saw Uncle Dockie and Tucson peering through the window. They had the look of fear on their faces. Aunt Marsha slowly turned and looked at them. I thought they might turn and run. Their eyes got big and round.

"Tucson, get in here right now!" demanded Aunt Marsha.

I could see him look sideways at Uncle Dockie. Uncle Dockie just shrugged his shoulders. Very slowly, Tucson inched into the room. They were on him in an instant. He was getting loved on by all three of them at the same time. He went from fear to liking where he was at that

C-Bar

moment. It was a good day to be Tucson.

Chapter 47
The Babb House

As the days passed, things calmed down. My house was a very happy place. Linda and Liz were thick as thieves. Every night they went to bed together. Sometimes, after Liz is asleep, Linda crawls under the covers with me. I think she likes me. From the sounds she is capable of making, I think she likes me a lot.

C-Bar

Chapter 48
Final Words

A few years ago, I came to this ranch and found something I had never found in the world. This ranch was an oasis in a world of people fighting and squabbling. I was a big city lawyer and made a living from this unfortunate quality we have. I hated every minute of it. This ranch sure ain't the city. The people here are a kind and loving bunch. If you have a problem, it's everyone's problem. No-one puts their needs ahead of others. I have become family here because I have laughed, cried, bled, failed, succeeded, celebrated and suffered with this wonderful family—all the things that seem necessary to form a bond. It's a strange part of life. It's necessary, in fact, to motivate us to grow. To bond with our fellow mankind is the only thing of real value that can't slip away. Bonding cannot happen if we think our needs are more important than the needs of others. Trust is only earned when people know you will never take advantage of them. Money and possessions can disappear because some far away politician decided he knows what is best for us. However, the bond a family has can't be so easily taken away.

I was told by a young man wise beyond his years, "You look back at all the hard times in life, and if you live long enough, you will at some point realize the hard times were the best part."

C-Bar

Mark Baugher

C-Bar

Happy Trails To You

If you are reading this, you must have read my story. I would love for you to email me back at markbaugher50@gmail.com and tell me who your favorite character is, or anything else you want to tell me. Just don't beat me up too much. I'm a sensitive guy, you know.

About the Author

Mark Baugher lives in Northern Arizona with his wife, Marcia, on a small rancho near the headwater of the Verde River. He is a Master Farrier, and when not under a horse, is riding one, exploring the Verde River, or treasure hunting in Sycamore Canyon.

C-Bar is Mr. Baugher's first novel. When Mark was asked about how he came to write *C-Bar*, his response was: "It's as if I didn't write this book. It poured out of me as if from some other person. I have no idea where it came from. People have asked me if I plan to write another C-Bar adventure. I tell them that I have no idea. I had no plan to write this one. Like the old saying goes: *People plan and God laughs.*"

Mark and Marcia live in a small adobe house surrounded by barns and shops. If you get out to the ranch, Marcia will answer the door with a big smile, and you'll feel like a youngster again, asking if Mark can come out and play.

Then you'll hear a welcoming voice from inside the house say: "You're just in time. I've got an extra horse saddled and waiting. I think I know where Geronimo's cave is hidden. We're wasting time, let's ride!"

And you will have the time of your life.

Made in the USA
Middletown, DE
06 May 2024